THE MAN
WHO BOUGHT
LONDON

THE MAN WHO BOUGHT LONDON

EDGAR WALLACE

Published by Hesperus Press Limited

28 Mortimer Street, London W1W 7RD

www.hesperuspress.com

The Man Who Bought London first published in 1915

First published by Hesperus Press Limited, 2015

Typeset by Roland Codd

Printed and bound by CPI Group (UK) Ltd, Croydon, CR0 4YY

ISBN: 978-1-84391-563-8

CHAPTER I

Night had come to the West End, but though the hour was late, though all Suburbia might at this moment be wrapped in gloom – a veritable desert of deadness relieved only by the brightness and animation of the busy public-houses – the Strand was thronged with a languid crowd all agape for the shady mysteries of the night world, which writers describe so convincingly, but the evidence of which is so often disappointing.

Deserted Suburbia had sent its quota to stare at the evil nightlife of the Metropolis. That it was evil none doubted. These pallid shop girls clinging to the arms of their protecting swains, these sedate, married ladies, arm in arm with their husbands, these gay young bloods from a thousand homes beyond the radius – they all knew the significance of those two words: 'West End'.

They stood for an extravagant aristocracy – you could see the shimmer and sheen of them as they bowled noiselessly along the Strand from theatre to supper table, in their brilliantly illuminated cars, all lacquer and silver work. They stood for all the dazzle of light, for all the joyous ripple of laughter, for the faint strains of music which came from the restaurants.

Suburbia saw, disapproved, but was intensely interested. For here was hourly proof of unthinkable sums that to the strolling pedestrians were only reminiscent of the impossible exercises in arithmetic which they had been set in their earlier youth. It all reeked of money – the Strand – Pall Mall (all ponderous and pompous clubs), but most of all, Piccadilly Circus, a great glittering diamond of light set in the golden heart of London.

Money – money – money! The contents bills reflected the spirit of the West. 'Well-known actress loses 20,000 pounds' worth of jewellery,' said one; 'Five million shipping deal,' said another, but that which attracted most attention was the naming bill which *The Monitor* had issued –

KING KERRY TO BUY LONDON
(Special)

It drew reluctant coppers from pockets which seldom knew any other variety of coinage than copper. It brought rapidly walking men, hardened to the beguilement of the contents-bill author, to a sudden standstill.

It even lured the rich to satisfy their curiosity. 'King Kerry is going to buy London,' said one man.

'I wish he'd buy this restaurant and burn it,' grumbled the other, rapping on the table with the handle of a fork. 'Waiter, how long are you going to keep me before you take my order?'

'In a moment, sir.'

A tall, good-looking man sitting at the next table, and occupying at the moment the waiter's full attention, smiled as he heard the conversation. His grey hair made him look much older than he was, a fact which afforded him very little distress, for he had passed the stage when his personal appearance excited much interest in his own mind. There were many eyes turned toward him, as, having paid his bill, he rose from his chair.

He seemed unaware of the attention he drew to himself, or, if aware, to be uncaring, and with a thin cigar between his even white teeth he made his way through the crowded room to the vestibule of the restaurant.

'By Jove,' said the man who had complained about the waiter's inattention, 'there goes the chap himself!' and he twisted round in his chair to view the departing figure.

'Who?' asked his friend, laying down the paper he had been reading.

'King Kerry,' said the other, 'the American millionaire.'

King Kerry strolled out through the revolving doors and was swallowed up with the crowd.

Following King Kerry, at a distance, was another well-dressed man, younger than the millionaire, with a handsome face and a subtle air of refinement.

He scowled at the figure ahead as though he bore him no good will, but made no attempt to overtake or pass the man in front, seeming content to keep his distance. King Kerry crossed to the Haymarket and walked down that sloping thoroughfare to Cockspur Street.

The man who followed was slimmer of build, yet well made. He walked with a curious restricted motion that was almost mincing. He lacked the swing of shoulder which one usually associated with the well-built man, and there was a certain stiffness in his walk which suggested a military training. Reflected by the light of a lamp under which he stopped when the figure in front slowed down, the face was a perfect one, small featured and delicate.

Hermann Zeberlieff had many of the characteristics of his Polish-Hungarian ancestry and if he had combined with these the hauteur of his aristocratic forebears, it was not unnatural, remembering that the Zeberlieffs had played no small part in the making of history.

King Kerry was taking a mild constitutional before returning to his Chelsea house to sleep. His shadower guessed this, and when King Kerry turned on to the Thames Embankment, the other kept on the opposite side of the broad avenue, for he had no wish to meet his quarry face to face.

The Embankment was deserted save for the few poor souls who gravitated hither in the hope of meeting a charitable miracle.

King Kerry stopped now and again to speak to one or another of the wrecks who ambled along the broad pavement, and his hand went from pocket to outstretched palm not once but many times.

There were some who, slinking towards him with open palms, whined their needs, but he was too experienced a man not to be able to distinguish between misfortune and mendicancy.

One such a beggar approached him near Cleopatra's Needle, but as King Kerry passed on without taking any notice of him, the outcast commenced to hurl a curse at him. Suddenly King Kerry turned back and the beggar shrunk towards the parapet as if expecting a blow, but the pedestrian was not hostile.

He stood straining his eyes in the darkness, which was made the more baffling because of the gleams of distant lights, and his cigar glowed red and grey.

'What did you say?' he asked gently. 'I'm afraid I was thinking of something else when you spoke.'

'Give a poor feller creature a copper to get a night's lodgin'!' whined the man. He was a bundle of rags, and his long hair and bushy beard were repulsive even in the light which the remote electric standards afforded.

'Give a copper to get a night's lodging?' repeated the other.

'An' the price of a dri– of a cup of coffee,' added the man eagerly.

'Why?'

The question staggered the night wanderer, and he was silent for a moment.

'Why should I give you the price of a night's lodging – or give you anything at all which you have not earned?'

There was nothing harsh in the tone: it was gentle and friendly, and the man took heart.

'Because you've got it an' I ain't,' he said – to him a convincing and unanswerable argument.

The gentleman shook his head.

'That is no reason,' he said. 'How long is it since you did any work?'

The man hesitated. There was authority in the voice, despite its mildness. He might be a 'split' – and it would not pay to lie to one of those busy fellows.

'I've worked orf an' on,' he said sullenly. 'I can't get work what with foreyners takin' the bread out of me mouth an' undersellin' us.'

It was an old argument, and one which he had found profitable, particularly with a certain type of philanthropist.

'Have you ever done a week's work in your life, my brother?' asked the gentleman.

One of the 'my brother' sort, thought the tramp, and drew from his armoury the necessary weapons for the attack.

'Well, sir,' he said meekly, 'the Lord has laid a grievous affliction on me head –'

The gentleman shook his head again.

'There is no use in the world for you, my friend,' he said softly. 'You occupy the place and breathe the air which might be better employed. You're the sort that absorbs everything and grows nothing: you live on the charity of working people who cannot afford to give you the hard-earned pence your misery evokes.'

'Are you goin' to allow a feller creature to walk about all night?' demanded the tramp aggressively.

'I have nothing to do with it, my brother,' said the other coolly. 'If I had the ordering of things I should not let you walk about.'

'Very well, then,' began the beggar, a little appeased.

'I should treat you in exactly the same way as I should treat any other stray dog – I should put you out of the world.'

And he turned to walk on.

The tramp hesitated for a moment, black rage in his heart. The Embankment was deserted – there was no sign of a policeman.

'Here!' he said roughly, and gripped King Kerry's arm.

Only for a second, then a hand like teak struck him under the jaw, and he went blundering into the roadway, striving to regain his balance.

Dazed and shaken he stood on the kerb watching the leisurely disappearance of his assailant. Perhaps if he followed and made a row the stranger would give him a shilling to avoid the publicity of the courts; but then the tramp was as anxious as the stranger, probably more anxious, to avoid publicity. To do him justice, he had not allowed his beard to grow or refrained from cutting his hair because he wished to resemble an anchorite, there was another reason. He would like to get even with the man who had struck him – but there were risks.

'You made a mistake, didn't you?'

The beggar turned with a snarl.

At his elbow stood Hermann Zeberlieff, King Kerry's shadower, who had been an interested spectator of all that had happened.

'You mind your own business!' growled the beggar, and would have slouched on his way.

'Wait a moment!' The young man stepped in his path. His hand went into his pocket, and when he withdrew it he had a little handful of gold and silver. He shook it; it jingled musically.

'What would you do for a tenner?' he asked.

The man's wolf eyes were glued to the money.

'Anything,' he whispered, 'anything, bar murder.'

'What would you do for fifty?' asked the young man.

'I'd – I'd do most anything,' croaked the tramp hoarsely.

'For five hundred and a free passage to Australia?' suggested the young man, and his piercing eyes were fixed on the beggar.

'Anything – anything!' almost howled the man.

The young man nodded.

'Follow me,' he said, 'on the other side of the road.'

They had not been gone more than ten minutes when two men came briskly from the direction of Westminster. They stopped every now and again to flash the light of an electric lamp upon the human wreckage which lolled in every conceivable attitude of slumber upon the seats of the Embankment. Nor were they content with this, for they scrutinized every passer-by – very few at this hour in the morning.

They met a leisurely gentleman strolling toward them, and put a question to him.

'Yes,' said he, 'curiously enough I have just spoken with him – a man of medium height, who spoke with a queer accent. I guess you think I speak with a queer accent too,' he smiled, 'but this was a provincial, I reckon.'

'That's the man, inspector,' said one of the two, turning to the other. 'Did he have a trick when speaking of putting his head on one side?'

The gentleman nodded.

'Might I ask if he is wanted – I gather that you are police officers?'

The man addressed hesitated and looked to his superior.

'Yes, sir,' said the inspector. 'There's no harm in telling you that his name is Horace Baggin, and he's wanted for murder – killed a warder of Devizes Gaol and escaped whilst serving the first portion of a lifer for manslaughter. We had word that he's been seen about here.'

They passed on with a salute, and King Kerry, for it was he, continued his stroll thoughtfully.

'What a man for Hermann Zeberlieff to find?' he thought, and it was a coincidence that at that precise moment the effeminate-looking Zeberlieff was entertaining an unsavoury tramp in his Park Lane study, plying him with a particularly villainous kind of vodka; and the tramp, with his bearded head on one side as he listened, was learning more about the pernicious ways of American millionaires than he had ever dreamt.

'Off the earth fellers like that ought to be,' he said thickly. 'Give me a chance – hit me on the jaw, he did, the swine – I'll millionaire him!'

'Have another drink,' said Zeberlieff.

CHAPTER II

The 'tube' lift was crowded, and Elsie Marion, with an apprehensive glance at the clock, rapidly weighed in her mind whether it would be best to wait for the next lift and risk the censure of Mr Tack or whether she should squeeze in before the great sliding doors clanged together. She hated lifts, and most of all she hated crowded lifts. Whilst she hesitated the doors rolled together with a 'Next lift, please!'

She stared at the door blankly, annoyed at her own folly. This was the morning of all mornings when she wished to be punctual.

Tack had been mildly grieved by her innumerable failings, and had nagged her persistently for the greater part of the week. She was unpunctual, she was untidy, she was slack to a criminal extent for a lady cashier whose efficiency is reckoned by the qualities which, as Tack insisted, she did not possess.

The night before, he had assembled the cash girls and had solemnly warned them that he wished to see them in their places at nine o'clock sharp. Not, he was at trouble to explain, at nine-ten, or at nine-five, not even at nine-one – but as the clock in the tower above Tack and Brighten's magnificent establishment chimed the preliminary quarters before booming out the precise information that nine o'clock had indeed arrived, he wished every lady to be in her place.

There had been stirring times at Tack and Brighten's during the past three months. An unaccountable spirit of generosity had been evinced by the proprietors – but it had been exercised towards the public rather than in favour of the unfortunate employees. The most extraordinary reductions in the sale price of their goods and the most cheeseparing curtailments of selling cost had resulted – so traitorous members of the counting-house staff said secretly – in a vastly increased turnover and, in some mysterious fashion, in vastly increased profits.

Some hinted that those profits were entirely fictitious, but that was slander only to be hinted at, for why should Tack and Brighten, a private company with no shareholders to please or pain, go out of their way to fake margins? For the moment, the stability of the firm was a minor consideration.

It wanted seven minutes to nine, and here was Elsie Marion at Westminster Bridge Road Tube Station, and Tack and Brighten's Oxford Street premises exactly twelve minutes away. She shrugged her pretty shoulders. One might as well be hanged for a sheep as a lamb, she thought. But she was angry with herself at her own stupidity. The next lift would be as crowded – she was left in no doubt as to that, for it was full as soon as the doors were open – and she might have saved three precious minutes.

She was crowded to the side of the lift and was thankful that the unsavoury and often uncleanly patrons of the line at this hour in the morning were separated from her by a tall man who stood immediately before her.

He was bareheaded, and his grey hair was neatly brushed and pomaded. His high forehead, clean-cut aquiline nose and firm chin, gave him an air of refinement and suggested breed. His eyes were blue and deep-set, his lips a trifle thin, and his cheek-bones, without being prominent, were noticeable on his sun-tanned face. All this she took in in one idle glance. She wondered who he was, and for what reason he was a traveller so early in the morning. He was well dressed, and a single black pearl in his cravat was suggestive of wealth. His hat he held between his two hands across his breast. He was an American, she gathered, because Americans invariably removed their hats in elevators when women were present.

The lift sank downward to the platform sixty feet below, and as it did she heard the faint sound of a 'ting', which told her she had missed a train. That would mean another three minutes' wait. She could have cried with vexation. It was a serious matter for her – an orphan girl absolutely alone in the world and dependent upon her own exertions for a livelihood. Cashiers were a drug on the market, and her shorthand and typewriting lessons had only advanced to a stage where she despaired of their getting any further.

Her salary was very small, and she thought regretfully of the days when she had spent more than that on shoes, before dear old spendthrift Aunt Martha had died, leaving her adopted daughter with no greater provision for the future than a Cheltenham education, a ten-pound note, and a massive brooch containing a lock from the head of Aunt Martha's love of the sixties.

Between the beginning of a lift's ascent and the moment the doors open again a girl with the cares of life upon her can review more than a man can write in a year. Before the giant elevator touched bottom Elsie Marion had faced the future and found it a little bleak. She was aware, as she turned to make her exit, that the tall man before her was watching her curiously. It was not the rude stare to which she had now grown callous, but the deeper, piercing glance of one who was genuinely interested. She suspected the inevitable smut on her nose, and fumbled for her handkerchief.

The stranger stepped aside to let her pass down first, and she was compelled to acknowledge the courtesy with a little nod. He followed her closely, instinct told her that; but so many people were following closely in that hurried slither to the platform.

There was some time to wait – two full minutes – and she strolled to the deserted end of the platform to get away from the crowd. She disliked crowds at all times, and this morning she hated them.

'Excuse me!'

She had heard that form of introduction before, but there was something in the voice which now addressed her which was unlike any of the impertinent overtures to which she had grown accustomed.

She turned and confronted the stranger. He was looking at her with a pleasant little smile.

'You'll think I'm crazy, I guess,' he said; 'but somehow I just had to come along and talk to you – you're scared of elevators?'

She might have frozen him – at least, she might have tried – but for some unaccountable reason she felt glad to talk to him. He was the kind of man she had known in the heyday of Aunt Martha's prosperity.

'I am a little scared,' she said, with a quick smile. 'It is absurd, because they are so safe.'

He nodded.

'I'm a little scared myself,' he confessed easily. 'Not that I'm afraid of dying, but when I think of the thousands of human beings whose future rests upon me and my life – why my hair goes up every time I cross the street.'

He was not asking her to be interested in himself. She felt that he was just voicing a thought that had occurred to him in a simple, natural way. She looked at him with greater interest.

'I've just been buying a lunatic asylum,' he said, and with an enquiring lift of his eyebrows, which at once asked permission and offered thanks when it was granted, he lit a cigar.

She stared at him and he laughed.

Whilst suspicion was gathering in her eyes, the train came hissing into the station.

The girl saw with dismay that it was crowded, and the mob which besieged each doorway was ten deep.

'You won't catch this,' said the man calmly. 'There'll be another in a minute.'

'I'm afraid I must try,' said the girl, and hurried along to where the surging throng were struggling to get aboard.

Her strange companion followed with long strides, but even with his assistance there was no chance of obtaining foothold, and she was left behind with a score of others. 'Time's money,' said the grey-haired stranger cheerfully. 'Don't be mean with it!'

'I can't afford to be anything else,' said the girl, pardonably exasperated. 'Possibly you haven't to face the wrath of an employer with a watch in his hand and doom on his face.'

She laughed a little in spite of her vexation.

'I'm so sorry,' she pleaded; 'but I did not intend allowing myself the luxury of a grumble about my worries – you were saying you have bought a lunatic asylum.'

He nodded, a twinkle in his eye.

'And you were thinking I had just escaped from one,' he said accusingly. 'Yes, I've just bought the Coldharbour Asylum – lock, stock, and barrel –'

She looked at him incredulously.

'Do you mean that?' she asked, and her scepticism was justified, for the Coldharbour Asylum is the largest in London, and the second largest in the world.

'I mean it,' he said. 'I am going to build the cutest residential club in London on that site.'

There was no time to say any more. Another train came in and, escorted by the grey-haired man, who in the shortest space of time had assumed a guardianship over her which was at once comforting and disconcerting, she found a seat in a smoking carriage. It was so easy to chat with him, so easy to confide hopes and fears which till that moment she had not put into words.

She found herself at Oxford Circus all too soon, and oblivious of the fact that the hands of the station clock pointed to twenty minutes after nine. 'A sheep as a lamb,' said her footsteps hollowly, as she went leisurely along the vaulted passageway to the lift.

'Were you going to Oxford Circus?' she asked, suddenly seized with a fear that she had taken this purchaser of lunatic asylums out of his way.

'Curiously enough, I was,' he said. 'I'm buying some shops in Oxford Street at half-past nine.'

Again she shot a swift glance at him, and he chuckled as he saw her shrink back a little.

'I am perfectly harmless,' he said mockingly.

They stepped out into Argyll Street together, and he offered his hand.

'I hope to meet you again,' he said, but did not tell her his name – it was King Kerry – though, he had read hers in the book she was carrying.

She felt a little uncomfortable, but gave him a smiling farewell. He stood for some time looking after her.

A man, unkempt, with a fixed, glassy look in his eye, had been watching the lift doors from the opposite side of the street. He started to cross as the grey-haired stranger made his appearance. Suddenly two shots rang out, and a bullet buzzed angrily past the grey man's face.

'That's yours, Mister!' howled a voice, and the next instant the owner was grabbed by two policemen.

A slow smile gathered at the corners of the grey-haired man's lips.

'Horace,' he said, and shook his head disapprovingly, 'you're a rotten shot!'

On the opposite side of Oxford Street, a man watched the scene from the upper window of a block of offices.

He saw the racing policemen, the huge crowd which gathered in a moment, and the swaying figures of the officers of the law and their half-mad prisoner. He saw, too, a grey-haired man, unharmed and calm, slowly moving away, talking with a sergeant of police who had arrived on the scene at the moment. The watcher shook a white fist in the direction of King Kerry.

'Some day, my friend!' he said between his clenched teeth, 'I will find a bullet that goes to its mark – and the girl from Denver City will be free!'

CHAPTER III

Mr Tack stood by the cashier's desk in the ready-made department. He wore upon his face the pained look of one who had set himself the pleasant task of being disagreeable, and yet feared the absence of opportunity.

'She won't come; we'll get a wire at eleven, saying she's ill, or her mother has been taken to the infirmary,' he said bitterly, and three sycophantic shop-walkers, immaculately attired in the most perfect fitting of frockcoats, who stood at a respectful distance, said in audible tones that it was really disgraceful.

They would have laughed at Mr Tack's comment on the sick mother, but they weren't sure whether he wanted them to laugh, because Mr Tack was a strict Churchman, and usually regarded sickness as part and parcel of the solemn ritual of life.

'She goes on Saturday week – whatever happens,' said Mr Tack grimly, and examined his watch. 'She would go at once if it wasn't for the fact that I can't get anybody to take her place at a minute's notice.' One of the shop-walkers, feeling by reason of his seniority of service that something was expected from him, remarked that he did not know what things were coming to.

It was to this unhappy group that Elsie Marion, flushed and a little breathless, came in haste from the stuffy dressing-room which Tack and Brighten's provided for their female employees.

'I'm so sorry!' she said, as she opened the glass-panelled door of the cash rostrum and swung herself up to the high stool.

Mr Tack looked at her. There he stood, as she had predicted, his gold chronometer in his hand, the doom on his face, an oppressive figure.

'Nine o'clock I was here, miss,' he said.

She made no reply, opening her desk, and taking out the check pads and the spikes of her craft.

'Nine o'clock I was here, miss,' repeated the patient Mr Tack — who was far from patient, being, in fact, in a white heat of temper.

'I'm very sorry!' she repeated.

A young man had strolled into the store, and since the officials responsible for piloting him to the counter of his desire were at that moment forming an admiring audience about Mr Tack, he was allowed to wander aimlessly. He was a bright boy, in a fawn dustcoat, and his soft felt hat was stuck on the back of his head. He had all the savoir faire and the careless confidence which is associated with one profession in the world – and one only. He drew nearer to the little group, having no false sense of modesty.

'You are sorry!' said Mr Tack with great restraint. He was a stout little man with a shiny bald head and a heavy, yellow moustache. 'You are sorry! Well, that's a comfort! You've absolutely set the rules – my rules – at defiance. You have ignored my special request to be here at nine o'clock – and you're sorry!'

Still the girl made no reply, but the young man in the soft felt hat was intensely interested.

'If I can get here, Miss Marion, you can get here!' said Mr Tack.

'I'm very sorry,' said the girl again. 'I overslept. As it is, I have come without any breakfast.'

'I could get up in time,' went on Mr Tack.

Elsie Marion turned on him, her patience exhausted. This was his way – he would nag from now till she left, and she wanted to see the end of it. She scented dismissal, anyway.

'What do you think I care,' she asked, stung to wrath, 'about what time you got up? You're horribly old compared to me;

22

you eat more than I, and you haven't my digestion. You get up because you can't sleep, probably. I sleep because I can't get up.'

It was a speech foreign to her nature, but she was stung to resentment.

Mr Tack was dumbfounded. Here were at least six statements, many of them unthinkably outrageous, which called for reprimand.

'You're discharged,' he snorted. The girl slipped down from her stool, very white of face.

'Not now – not now!' said Mr Tack hastily. 'You take a week's notice from Saturday.'

'I'd rather go now,' she said quietly.

'You'll stay to suit my convenience,' breathed Mr Tack, 'and then you will be discharged without a character.'

She climbed back to her stool, strangely elated.

'Then you've got to stop nagging me,' she said boldly. 'I'll do whatever it is my duty to do, but I won't be bullied. I don't want your linen-draper's sarcasms,' she went on recklessly, encouraged by the sympathetic smile of the young man in the soft felt hat, who was now an unabashed member of the audience, 'and I won't have your ponderous rebukes. You are the head of a beastly establishment in which your hirelings insult defenceless girls who dare not resent. One of these days I'm going to take the story of Tack and Brighten to *The Monitor*.'

It was a terrible threat born of a waning courage, for the girl was fast losing her exhilaration which came to her in her moment of temporary triumph; but Mr Tack, who was no psychologist, and did not enquire into first causes, turned pink and white. Already *The Monitor* had hinted at scandal in 'a prosperous sweating establishment in Oxford Street', and Mr Tack had the righteous man's fear of publicity.

'You – you dare!' he spluttered. 'You – you be careful, Miss – I'll have you out of here, by Jove! Yes – neck and crop! What can we do for you, sir?'

He turned sharply to the young man in the trilby hat, having observed him for the first time.

'My name's Gillett,' said the youth bluntly, 'and I am a representative of *The Monitor* – er – I want to see this young lady for two minutes.'

'Go to the devil!' said Mr Tack defiantly.

The young man bowed.

'After I have interviewed this young lady,' he said.

'I forbid you to give this man information about my business,' exploded the enraged partner.

The reporter closed his eyes wearily.

'My poor fellow,' he said, shaking his head, 'it isn't about your business I want to see this lady, it's about King Kerry.'

Mr Tack opened his mouth in astonishment.

'Mr King Kerry?' he said. 'Why, that's the gentleman who is buying this business!'

He blurted it out – a secret which he had so jealously guarded. He explained in one sentence the reason for the economies, the sales at less than cost, the whole disastrous and nefarious history of the past months.

'Buying this business, is he?' said Gillett, unimpressed. 'Why, that's nothing! He was nearly murdered at Oxford Circus Tube Station half an hour ago, and he's bought Portland Place Mansions since then.'

He turned to the alarmed girl.

'Told me to come along and find you,' he said. 'Described you so that I couldn't make any mistake.'

'What does he want?' she asked, shaking.

'Wants you to come to lunch at the Savoy,' said Mr Gillett, 'and tell him whether Tack and Brighten's is worth buying at the price.'

Mr Tack did not swoon, he was too well trained. But as he walked to his private office he swayed unsteadily, and the shop-walker in the Ribbon Department, who was a member of the Anti-Profanity League, heard what Mr Tack was saying to himself, and put his fingers in his ears.

CHAPTER IV

A bewildered man sat in a cell at Vine Street, his aching head between his large, grimy hands. He was trying, in his dull brutish way, to piece together the events of the previous night and of that morning. He remembered that he had met a man on the Thames Embankment. A gentleman who had spoken coldly, whose words had cut like a steel knife, and yet who had all the outward evidence of benevolence. And then that this man had struck him, and there had come another, a smooth-faced, young-looking man, who had taken him to a house and given him a drink.

The stranger had led him to a place, and told him to watch, and they had followed this grey-haired man through streets in a taxi-cab.

Horace Baggin had never ridden in a motor car of any description before, and he remembered this. He remembered all that had happened through a thin alcoholic haze. They had gone to South London and then they had come back, and the man had left him at a tube station with a pistol. Presently the grey-haired man had made his appearance, and Baggin, mad with artificial rage, unthinking, unreasoning, had stepped forward and shot wildly, and then the police had come. That was all.

Suddenly a thought struck him, and he started up with an oath. He was wanted for that other affair in Wiltshire. Would they recognize him? He pressed a little electric bell, which was placed in the wall of the cell, and the turnkey came and surveyed him gravely through the grating.

'What is the charge?' Baggin asked eagerly.

'You know what the charge is,' said the other; 'it was read over to you in the charge-room.'

'But I have forgotten,' said the man sullenly. 'It won't hurt you to tell me what I am charged with, will it?'

The officer hesitated. Then –

'You are charged with attempted murder and with manslaughter.'

'What manslaughter?' asked Baggin quickly.

'Oh, an old affair, you know, Baggin!'

'Baggin!'

So they knew his name.

Well, there was one gleam of hope, one chance for him. This rich stranger who had lured him out to shoot the grey-haired man, he could help. He was a toff, he was; he lived in a grand house.

What was his name?

Baggin paced his cell for some quarter of an hour, racking his aching brain for the name which eluded him. Yes, curiously enough, he had seen the name, though the other might not have suspected the fact. In the hallway of the house to which the stranger took him was a tiny stand with glass and silver things, fragile and dainty, on which, as they had entered, Baggin had seen some letters addressed to the man, and he, naturally curious, and gifted moreover with the ability to read handwriting, had deciphered the name as – as – Zeberlieff!

That was the name, 'Zeberlieff', and Park Lane, too – the house was in Park Lane. He remembered it now. He was elated at the result of his thought, a little exhausted too.

He called the gaoler again, and the weary official obeyed, not without resentment.

'What do you want now?' he asked bitterly.

'Can you let me have a sheet of paper, an envelope and a pencil?'

'I can,' said the gaoler. 'Who do you want to write to – a lawyer?'

'That's it,' said Baggin. 'He is my own private lawyer,' he said proudly. 'A regular "nut" he is, too; he won't half put it across you people if you don't behave properly.'

'Not so much lip!' said the gaoler, and went away, to return in a few moments with the necessary vehicles of communication.

He passed them through the open grating in the door, and Horace sat down to the unaccustomed task of composing a letter, which was not incriminating to his employer, but which conveyed to him a sense of his responsibility, and the danger in which he stood if he did not offer the succour which was required of him.

'Honoured Sir,' the letter ran (it would serve no useful purpose to faithfully expose the liberties he took with the English language), *'some time ago I did a job of work for you. I am now in great trouble having shot the gentleman, and I should be very much obliged if you would assist me to the best of your ability.'*

It was a noteworthy contribution to the literature of artfulness. Horace Baggin had been inspired to remember Zeberlieff as an old employer in the mythical period when Horace Baggin preferred hard work to the illicit calling which had ended so disastrously for him.

'Zeberlieff,' said the gaoler as he read the address and scanned the letter; 'why, that's an American millionaire, ain't it?'

'That's so,' said Horace Baggin complacently; 'he's been a good friend of mine. I used to be his' – he hesitated – 'his game-keeper,' he said. 'He had an estate down our way,' he went on grimly. 'Very good shot, too.'

'I will send it down if you like,' said the gaoler; 'though he will probably only give you the cold shoulder. You know when a man gets into trouble he can't expect his old master to come prancing round getting him out. Not in these days, anyway.'

Nevertheless, he sent it on at Baggin's request.

After that effort of thought and diplomacy Horace Baggin felt at peace with the world. In the afternoon he was called before the magistrate. Formal evidence was taken, and he was remanded for one day and removed back to the cell; that meant another day at the police court.

Well, he was prepared to face it. It was not the first time he had been in trouble, but it was the first time he had been in a position where, in spite of the enormity of the crime, hope had extended so rosy a vista of possibilities. He had received news that his letter had been delivered, and waited hopefully for his partner in crime to make a move. It was fine, he thought, to have such a pal. The prospect of succour had almost entirely eclipsed the seriousness of the charges which the man had to face.

Morning found Baggin more sober and more bitter. So this sweet pal of his had gone back on him, had made no attempt to answer his call of distress, even though the imprisoned man had made it apparent that no immediate danger threatened the confederate. Well, there was another way out of it, another way in which he might excuse his conduct and find himself the centre of a sensational case. He waited till the gaoler passed, and then –

'I want to see the inspector in charge of this case,' he said. 'I have got a statement to make.'

'Right-o!' said the gaoler. 'You had better have your breakfast first. You will be one of the first to go into court, you know.'

Baggin nodded.

'Coffee and toast have been sent in for you.'

'Who by?' asked Baggin, with some show of interest.

'One of your pals,' said the gaoler, and vouchsafed no further information.

So Zeberlieff had moved, had he?

Baggin had no pals, save the pal for whom he was waiting, and in whom he had placed his faith. His spirits rose again. He remembered that it would be as well not to be too emphatic. There might come a time when it would be necessary to admit the existence of the other man.

'Here is your breakfast,' said a detective, as the door swung open again, and he was accompanied by a warder with a little tray, carrying a steaming jug of coffee and a plate of toast. 'Now, just think it out, and let me know how you feel before you go into court. It might make all the difference in the world to you. Why should you stand the racket for another man's crime?' the detective asked.

Baggin was not to be cajoled, but no sooner had the door closed behind the detective than he moved mechanically across to where the writing pad lay and picked it up. He would give the stranger a chance; in the meantime he was hungry.

He took a draught of the coffee, at the same time wondering how his newfound pal would get him out of the scrape.

Five minutes later a detective and the gaoler strolled down to his cell.

'I will have a talk with him,' said the detective, and the gaoler, without troubling to look through the grating, inserted the key and pulled the door open.

The detective uttered an exclamation and sprang into the cell. Baggin lay in a huddled heap amongst a litter of broken china and spilt coffee. The detective lifted him up bodily and turned him over.

'My God!' he said, 'he's dead! He has been poisoned! There is the scent of cyanide of potassium in this cell.'

'Poisoned?' asked the startled gaoler. 'Who did it? How did he get it?'

'It was in the coffee,' replied the detective slowly, 'and the man that sent it in was the man who employed Baggin to do his dirty work.'

CHAPTER V

Before the lunch hour arrived at Tack and Brighten's, there came to Elsie Marion, through the medium of the senior shop-walker, an invitation to attend upon Mr Tack. It was couched in such elegant language, and delivered with grace that no doubt could exist in the mind of any intelligent being that message and messenger had been most carefully rehearsed.

At five minutes to one Elsie presented herself at the partners' office. Mr Tack was not alone; his partner sat bunched up in a chair, biting his knuckles and scowling furiously.

The firm of Tack and Brighten was not distinguished by the fact that one member of the firm whose name appeared upon the facade had no incorporate existence. There may have been a Brighten in the old days, but nobody had ever seen him or met him. He was a business legend. The dominant partner of the firm was James Leete.

He was a stout man, stouter than the fiery Mr Tack. He walked with a waddle, and his face was not pleasant. It was creased and puffed into a score of unhealthy rolls and crevices; his nose was red and bulbous and to accentuate and emphasize his unloveliness, he wore a black-rimmed monocle. Immensely rich, he fawned a way through life, for he sought inclusion in ducal house parties and was happiest in the society of rank.

'This is the girl?' he asked.

He had a thick, husky voice, naturally coarse, through which ran with grotesque insistence a tone of mock culture which he had acquired by conscientious imitation of his models.

'This is Miss Marion,' said Tack gloomily.

Leete leered up at him.

'Pretty girl! I suppose you know it, Miss What's-your-name?'

Elsie made no reply, though the colour came to her cheek at the undisguised insolence of the man.

'Now, look here!' – Leete swung his gross shape round on the revolving chair till he faced her and wagged a fat finger in her direction – 'you've got to be very careful what you say to my friend King Kerry: everything you tell him he'll repeat to me, and if you tell one solitary, single lie about this business I can have you clapped into gaol for criminal libel.'

The girl smiled in spite of herself.

'You can grin!' growled Leete; 'but I mean it – see? Not that you know anything that we mind you saying. You're not exactly in the confidence of the firm – and if you were,' he added quickly, 'you'd know no more to our detriment than you do.'

'Don't worry!' answered the girl coolly. 'I shall tell him nothing except that you have said you are a friend of his.'

'It's not necessary to tell him that,' said Leete hastily.

'I think it is only fair to him to know what awful things people are saying about him,' said Elsie sweetly. She was in her 'sheep and lamb' mood, and she was very hungry. Later she was to marvel at her courage and her impertinence, but just at the moment she was conscious of nothing so much as a terrible sense of absence in the region of her little diaphragm.

'My girl,' said Leete slowly, 'I don't enquire as to how you got to know my friend Kerry, and I won't enquire, and I won't hint –'

'You'd jolly well better not!' flared the girl, her eyes shining angrily; 'because as I'm feeling just now I'd throw this inkstand at your head for two pins!'

Mr Leete pushed his chair back in alarm as the girl lifted the inkwell from the table and gripped it suggestively.

'Don't misunderstand me!' he begged with a warding arm raised. 'I'm only talking to you for your good. I want to see you get on. I'll tell you what I've suggested, Miss Marion: we keep you on, we double your salary, and we put you in charge of the checking department.'

For one moment only the magnificence of the offer overcame her. A larger room – the little luxuries which on her old salary were impossible –

'And,' added Mr Leete impressively, 'a bonus of a hundred pounds the day this business is transferred to its new proprietor.'

'A hundred pounds!' she repeated.

She put down the inkwell: it was out of place under the circumstances.

'And what would you ask me to do for this?' she demanded.

'Nothing,' put in Tack, a silent spectator till now.

'You shut up, Tack!' snarled the partner. 'Yes, of course, we want something: we want you to tell Mr Kerry all the good you can about the firm.'

She understood now.

'That will take me exactly half a second,' said Elsie.

Her duty was clear. They were binding her to lie. She had not taken Gillett's message seriously. She had not even grasped the elementary fact that the grey-haired stranger in the tube was the great King Kerry, multi-millionaire and controller of billions. Her head was whirling with the happenings of the day – she was intoxicated by novelty, and only the natural and buoyant healthy outlook of the girl kept her any way near to normal.

Leete took stock of her and wondered he had not noticed her before. She was a beautiful girl with her fine grey eyes, and the mass of hair that half-framed her face in a cloud of russet gold.

The hands were small and shapely, the figure slender and straight. Even the unattractive uniform which Messrs Tack and Brighten insisted upon their girls wearing did not detract from her beauty. Now, with faint shadows which an insufficiency of sleep and a lack of food had painted beneath her eyes, she was ethereal and rather adorable. So thought Mr Leete, no mean judge, and he stroked his bristly grey-black moustache reflectively.

She half turned to the door.

'You will not require me any more?' she asked.

'Remember!' Again Leete was shaking his ridiculous finger at her. 'Criminal libel means imprisonment.'

'I don't feel like laughing this morning,' said Elsie Marion; 'but you are tempting me awfully.'

She closed the door behind her before Mr Leete had time to express his wishes about her eyes, her soul, and her obscure relations. For Mr Leete had no respect for anybody whose name was not in Burke's *Landed Gentry*.

She turned up to the dressing-room and found herself besieged by an admiring crowd of girls, for the news that Miss Marion had 'cheeked' Tack and lived to tell the tale was common property.

She repressed a natural and human inclination to reveal the fact that she was lunching at the Savoy, and fled from the building before she betrayed her great secret.

Mr Kerry was waiting in the entrance hall of the hotel alone. It seemed to the girl that every eye in the great vestibule was focused on him and in this surmise she was probably right, for a billionaire is something out of the ordinary; but a billionaire who had escaped assassination at the hands of a former 'friend', and whose name, in consequence, was on every evening newspaper placard in London, was most wonderful of all.

Throughout the meal, taken at a table overlooking the river, they talked on a variety of subjects. He was an especially well-read man, with a penchant for the Persian poets, and was a delighted and unconventionally demonstrative man – leaning across the table to stroke her hand – when she capped a couplet from Hafiz with a verse from Sadi –

'Though we are straws laid down to warm the sod, We once were flowers in the eyes of God.'

'Excellent! splendid!' he cried. 'I don't remember that rendering of the poem.'

'It is a rendering I made myself,' she confessed. She had seen a translation and had improved upon it.

They meandered through the most delicious lunch Elsie had eaten since the extravagant days of Aunt Martha. He encouraged her to talk of that relative. 'A fine woman,' he called her enthusiastically. 'I love these people who spend all their money.'

She shook her head laughingly.

'That is not your creed, Mr Kerry,' she challenged.

'It is – it is!' he said eagerly; 'here is my parable of finance. Money is water. The sea is the wealth of the nations. It is evaporated and drawn up to the sky and is sprinkled upon the earth. For some of us it runs in deep channels, and if we are skilful we can dam it for our use. Some of us dam it deeply, and some shallowly. With some it just filters away and is swallowed up, only to reappear in somebody else's dam.'

She nodded. It was a new imagery, and the conceit pleased her.

'If you keep it stagnant it is no use,' he went on, as eager as a boy. 'You must let it pass along, always keeping a reserve; it shouldn't run out faster than it runs in. I have a big dam – high up on the hills it stands; a great and mighty reservoir always filling, always running off. Farther down the hill hundreds of other men are collecting the waste from my overflow; farther down smaller men with smaller dams, and so on – till it runs away to the sea, as it must in time, to the great ocean of world-wealth which collects everything and gives back everything.'

She looked at him in amazement, this man who had escaped death by an inch and was so absorbed in his philosophy of wealth that he had forgotten how near he had stood to the brink of eternity, and her heart warmed to this courageous man.

He came to earth quickly, fished in his inside pocket and produced a fat little book with a soiled leather cover. He placed it tenderly on the table and opened it. It was a book which had been in use for years. Some of the pages were covered with minute writings, some had become detached and had been carefully fastened in again.

'I owe you an explanation,' he said, and sorted from a few loose papers a photograph. He looked at it for a moment and laid it on the table for the girl to see.

She gave a gasp.

'Why, that is me!' she said, and looked at him in amazement.

'It is rather like you, isn't it?' He replaced the photograph, his lips pressed tight together. 'As a matter of fact it isn't you; some time you shall know who it is – that is,' he smiled again, 'if I am not the victim of an imitator of the late Horace –'

'Late?' she repeated.

The other nodded gravely.

'He took cyanide of potassium in his cell at Marlborough Street,' he said, 'leaving his good work for his employer to carry on. What time have you to be back?' he asked suddenly.

'Two o'clock,' she said in a sudden panic, for no great reason.

'It's now three,' he said. 'You need not go back till four.'

'But, Mr Tack —'

'I am the head of the firm,' he smiled. 'I have bought Tack and Brighten's – closed the deal on the phone just before you arrived. I have taken the liberty of raising your wages to fifteen pounds a week. Shall I order you another coffee?'

Elsie opened her mouth to say 'yes', but no sound came. For the first time in her life she was at a loss for words.

CHAPTER VI

Though all the world now knows of King Kerry, and his life and achievements are inscribed more or less accurately in the scrappy works of reference which are so popular nowadays, only a privileged few know of the inception of the great Trust which came to London in 19—.

It came about indirectly as a result of the Shearman Anti-Trust Law which caused wholesale resignations from the boards of American companies, and drove what is known on the other side of the Atlantic as the 'mergers' out of business. These were Trust men who had done nothing in their lives but combine conflicting business interests into one great monopoly. They found themselves scarcely within the pale of the law – they found, too, that their opportunities were limited. These men had dealt in millions. They had liquid assets, hard cash ready for employment at a moment's notice. They came in a body to England – the eight greatest financiers of the United States. Bolscombe E. Grant rented Tamby Hall from the Earl of Dichester; Thomas A. Logge (the Wire King) settled in London; Gould Lampest bought an estate in Lincolnshire; and the others – Verity Sullivan, Combare Lee, Big Jack Simms, and King Kerry – settled down in London.

There were others who joined forces with them; but they were unimportant. Cagely H. Smith put a million into the pool, but backed out after the Orange Street affair. The eight dispensed with his million without noticing that it had gone. He was a little man, and they made clear, for when Cagely tried to sneak back into the pool, offering not only the five million dollars he had originally staked, but half a million pounds in addition as evidence of his faith, his overtures were rejected. Another small man was

Morris Lochmann, who subscribed roughly 600,000 pounds – and there were several of his kind. The 'L Trust', as it called itself, was autocratic to a degree. Men who came in with inflated ideas as to their importance were quashed as effectively as a fly is swotted. Hermann Zeberlieff was one of these. He was a big man in a small place, one of the little kings of industry, who measured themselves by the standard of local publicity. He threw some 1,200,000 pounds into the pool – but he talked. The fever for notoriety was so strong in him that he committed the unpardonable crime of having a photograph of 'this mammoth cheque' (so the letterpress typed on the back of the picture called it) sent to all the papers.

The cheque was never presented. He had jeopardized the success of the project by alarming a public too ready to be scared by one of two words – 'trust' and 'conscription'.

Zeberlieff was a large holder of United Western Railway stock. On the morning the photograph appeared the stock stood at £23 per share in the market. By the next afternoon it had beaten down to £12 10s. On the following day it slumped to £8 – a sensational drop. The most powerful group in the world had 'beared' it. Hermann crawled out of the mess with a loss of £800,000.

'What can I do?' he wailed to Bolscombe Grant, that gaunt man of money.

'I guess the best thing you can do,' said Mr Grant, chewing the end of his cigar thoughtfully, 'is to send a picture of yourself to the papers.'

It was the first hint to Hermann Zeberlieff that he was the subject of disciplinary measures.

It was typical of the Trust that it made no attempt to act collectively in the sense that it was guided by a majority. It delegated all its powers to one man, gave him a white card to scribble liabilities; neither asked for explanations nor expected them. They found the money, and they placed it at the disposal of King Kerry because King Kerry was the one man of their number who understood the value of real estate properties. They worked on a simple basis. The rateable value of London was £45,000,000. They computed that London's income was £150,000,000 a year. They were satisfied that with the expenditure of £50,000,000 they could extract ten per cent of London's income.

That was roughly the idea, and to this was added the knowledge that vast as was the importance of the metropolis, it had only reached the fringe of its possibilities. London would one day be twice its present size, and ground value would be enormously increased. Its unique situation, the security which came from the geographic insularity of England and the strength of its navy, the feeding quality of its colonies, all combined to mark London as a world capital.

'I see London extended to St. Albans on the north, Newbury on the west, and Brighten on the south,' wrote King Kerry in his diary. 'It may even extend to Colchester on the east; but the east side of any township is always an unknown quantity in a scheme of development.'

There were difficulties to overcome, almost insuperable difficulties, but that was part of the game and made the players keener. Patience would do much: judicious pressure tactfully applied would do more.

King Kerry wanted to buy the big block of buildings comprising Goulding's Universal Stores. Goulding's stood out, so Kerry bought the next block, which was Tack and Brighten's.

Elsie Marion presented herself at ten o'clock punctually at the modest suite of offices which the 'L Trust' occupied in

Glasshouse Street. It was unusual that a great financial corporation should be habited so far west, but a peculiarity of the Trust and its operations was the fact that never once did it attempt to handle property in the area between Temple Bar and Aldgate Pump. It was not in the scheme of King Kerry to disturb conditions in the City of London itself.

The office in Glasshouse Street occupied the ground floor of a modern block. The floors above were let out to an insurance company, a firm of solicitors, and an estate agent – all firms of undoubted integrity, and all, moreover, largely associated with the working of the Trust.

The girl had read something of this office in the newspapers. A flippant evening journal had christened it 'The Jewel House', because it bore some resemblance to the famous store of Britain's treasures in the Tower of London. In her desire to be punctual she had arrived a quarter of an hour before the appointed time, and she had leisure to inspect the remarkable facade. A small brass plate against the entrance gave the seeker after information the news that this was the registered office of the 'L Financial Corporation, Limited', for a small company with a ridiculous capital had been registered as a matter of expediency. The company owned the building in which it was situated and little more, but it served as a cover for everyday purposes. It supplied an office and a repository for the documents of larger concerns, and, by the very publicity it afforded, effectively veiled the private transactions of its select shareholders.

The windows of the office reached to the ground. They were made of three huge sheets of plate-glass set roughly bow-shaped between solid brass pillars. Before them were three screens of large-meshed steel netting, held in their place by pillars of gun-metal.

It was this which inspired the reference to 'The Jewel House', for here the resemblance ended. Yet the interior of the front office was remarkable. It was bare of furnishing. A blood-red carpet covered the floor, and in the centre, supported by a square pedestal of granite which ran up from the basement, was a big safe. Apparently, it rested on the floor, but no ordinary floor could support the weight of metal, and the central pedestal had been put in whilst the building was in course of erection.

Nor was this the only remarkable feature of the room.

The walls were completely covered by lengths of mirror, two of which were set at an angle in the far corners of the room. Add six arc lamps depending upon independent supplies, and hung so that their rays fell upon the safe at every aspect and burning day and night, and you have some idea of this unique department which attracted all London and became one of the sights of the metropolis.

Day or night, the passer-by had a full view of the safe, and no man entered that room save King Kerry and the armed guard which watched the cleaners at their work every morning.

Even in the clear light of day it was an impressive sight, and Elsie entered the building a little awe-stricken. She was taken to the back office by a uniformed commissionaire and found the grey-haired young man alone in his office, writing. He jumped up as she came in and pulled forward a luxurious chair.

'Sit down, Miss Marion,' he said. 'I shall be calling you Elsie soon, because' – he smiled at the little flush that came to her cheek – 'in America, why, I guess we're more friendly to our business associates than you are in this country.'

He pushed a button and the commissionaire came in.

'Are your two comrades outside?' he asked.

'Yes, sir,' said the man.

'Tell them to come in.'

A few seconds later the man returned, bringing two other commissionaires. They stood stiffly by the door.

'This is Miss Marion,' said King Kerry, and the girl rose.

The men scrutinized her seriously.

'Do you mind standing over by the wall?' asked Kerry.

She obediently walked across the room as Kerry switched on all the lights.

'You will know Miss Marion now,' said Kerry, 'in whatever light she appears. She is to have access to this office day or night. That is all.'

The men saluted and withdrew as Kerry extinguished the electric bulbs.

'I'm sorry to bother you,' he said; 'but since you are the only other person in the world who will have this privilege, it is necessary that I should be very thorough. These men are in charge of the guards, and one of them is on duty day and night.'

She seated herself again with a pleasurable sense of importance.

'May I ask you one question?' she said.

He nodded.

'Why have you chosen me? I am not a proficient secretary, and you know nothing whatever about me. I may be an associate of the worst characters.'

He leant back in a padded chair, surveying her quizzically.

'All that I know about you,' he said, 'is that you are the daughter of the Rev. George Marion, a widower, who died seven years ago and left you little more than would carry you to your aunt in London. That you have an uncle in America, who is

raising a large family and innumerable mortgages in the middle
west; that you had a brother who died in childhood; and that you
have been engaged by three firms – Meddlesohn, of Eastcheap
– you left them because you refused to be party to a gross fraud;
Highlaw and Sons, of Moorgate Street – which you left because
the firm failed; and Tack and Brighten – which you would have
left, anyway.'

She stared at him in amazement.

'How did you find this out?'

'My dear child,' he said, rising and laying a fatherly hand upon
her shoulder, 'how does one find things out? By asking the
people who know. I take few risks; I came down to Southwark to
see you, and if possible to speak to you before I engaged you or
you knew that I wanted to engage you. Now!'

He returned to his desk briskly.

'This is business. You receive fifteen pounds weekly from me
and a bonus at the end of every year. Your duty is to act as my
confidante, to write letters – not as I shall dictate them, for I hate
dictating – but in the sense of my instructions.'

She nodded.

'There is one other thing,' he said, and lowered his voice as
he leant across the desk. 'I want you to remember three words.'

She waited, expecting a conventional little motto which
pointed out the way of efficiency.

'Those three words,' he went on in the same tone, 'must never
be uttered to a living soul whilst I am alive; must be repeated to
nobody but myself.'

Elsie felt incapable of being further amazed than she was. The
last twenty-four hours had held, so it seemed to her, the very
limit of surprises.

'To my partners, to my friends, or to my enemies – and especially to my enemies,' he continued with a fleeting smile, 'you must never employ them – until I am dead. Then, in the presence of the gentlemen who are connected with this corporation you shall say' – he dropped his voice to a whisper – 'you shall say, "Kingsway needs Paving."'

'"Kingsway needs Paving,"' she repeated in a whisper.

'Whatever happens do not forget those words,' he said gravely. 'Repeat them to yourself till you know them as you know your own name.'

She nodded again. Bewildered as she was, half inclined to laugh, with the old suspicion as to his sanity recurring, she knew that immense issues hung upon those meaningless words – 'Kingsway needs Paving'.

CHAPTER VII

At the moment when Elsie was being initiated into the mysteries of King Kerry's office, two men sat at breakfast in the sumptuous dining room of Mr Leete's flat in Charles Street.

One of these was the redoubtable Leete himself, in a dressing-gown of flowered silk, and the other the young-looking Mr Hermann Zeberlieff. He was a man of thirty-eight, but had one of those faces which defy the ravages of time and the consequence of excess.

Leete and he were friends. They had met in Paris in the days when Millionaire Zeberlieff's name was in every paper as the man who had cornered wheat.

They had something in common, these two men, and when a Wall Street syndicate had smashed the corner, ruining hundreds of small speculators, but leaving Hermann Zeberlieff ten times over a dollar millionaire, Leete had accompanied the young man on the yachting cruise which the execration of the American public and the virulence of the Press had made advisable, and the friendship ripened.

Later Millionaire Zeberlieff was to court publicity more disastrously to himself, and the operations of the 'L Trust' were to rob him of half his fortune. They were talking of money now. It was a subject which absorbed both men.

'You're a pretty rich man yourself, aren't you, Leete?'

Zeberlieff put the question in a tone that suggested that he was not particular whether he was answered or not.

'Fairly,' admitted the unprepossessing Mr Leete.

'A millionaire?'

Leete nodded.

'Then why the devil did you sell Kerry your store?' asked the other in astonishment.

Mr Leete's face puckered into a grin.

'There was a bigger store next door,' he said cheerfully. 'Goulding's were doing twice the trade – taking all our customers, and prospering. They've got the best position – street corner and a double show of shop fronts. That's why!'

'But why hasn't he bought Goulding's?'

The smile on Mr Leete's face was expressive.

'Goulding's won't sell. He bought the land and is ground landlord, but he can't disturb Goulding's because they've eighty years' lease to run.'

Zeberlieff whistled.

'That will upset him,' he said with satisfaction.

'As a matter of fact, Tack and Brighten's is a dying concern,' Mr Leete went on frankly. 'Unless he can buy Goulding's he's as good as lost his money. Goulding's will sell – at a price.'

He winked.

'By the way,' he said suddenly, 'did you hear that Kerry had been attacked in the public street – shot at?' The other nodded. 'Well, the man that shot at him is dead!'

Zeberlieff raised his eyebrows.

'Indeed!'

Mr Leete nodded.

'Apparently he was mad drunk when he got to the station, and when one of his pals sent him in a mug of coffee the police let him have it – thought it would sober him.'

'And did it?' asked the other without any great show of interest.

Mr Leete nodded again.

'It killed him – cyanide of potassium in the coffee. My doctor,' he paused and raised his voice ever so little, 'my doctor, Sir John Burcheston, who happened to be passing, was called in, and he told me all about it.'

'Extraordinary!' said Mr Zeberlieff, obviously bored. 'How did it get to him?'

'I don't know – they found the boy who brought the coffee, but he says he was sent by a stranger who can't be found.'

'Sounds thrilling,' said Zeberlieff coolly.

'Thought you'd be interested,' said the other.

'I'm more interested in your deal with Kerry. Didn't he know that Goulding's wouldn't sell?' asked Zeberlieff incredulously; 'it doesn't seem possible!'

'He thinks he has got a bargain,' chuckled the other. 'We knocked the prices down and put the profits up – your Trust folk aren't as clever as they pretend.'

But Zeberlieff shook his head. 'If you underrate the ability of the "Big L",' he said seriously, 'you're going to nose trouble – that's all. King Kerry smells the value of property just as crows scent carrion: he doesn't make mistakes.'

Leete looked up at the other, showing his yellow teeth in a sneer.

'If I'm speaking disparagingly of a friend of yours –' he began.

The plump baby-face of Zeberlieff went a dull red and his eyes glittered ominously.

'A friend of mine?' he cried savagely. 'A friend of mine – Leete, I hate that man so much that I'm afraid of myself! I hate the look of him and the sound of his voice: I hate him, and yet he fascinates me.'

He strode rapidly up and down the long room.

'Do you know,' he asked, stopping suddenly in his walk, 'that I often follow him for hours on end – dog his footsteps literally, for no other reason than because I hate him so much that I cannot let him out of my sight?' His face was pale now; his hands, moist with perspiration, were clenched till the knuckles showed whitely. 'You think I'm mad – but you don't know the fascination of hate. I hate him, my God, how I hate him!'

He hissed the last words between his clenched teeth. Mr Leete nodded approvingly. 'Then I'm going to give you good news,' he said slowly. 'Kerry is going to be bled.'

'Bled?' There was no mistaking the almost brutal joy in the other's tone.

'Not the way you mean,' said Mr Leete facetiously; 'but we're going to make him pay for Goulding's.'

'We?'

'We,' repeated Leete. 'My dear man, Goulding's is mine – has always been my business. I built up Goulding's out of Tack and Brighten. I have sold the failure; I have kept the success.'

Again Zeberlieff frowned.

'Kerry didn't know?' he asked, his incredulity apparent.

Mr Leete shook his head, and laughed – he laughed a curiously high laugh, almost falsetto. Zeberlieff waited until he had finished.

'I'd like to bet you all the money in the world he did know,' he said, and the smile vanished from Mr Leete's homely face.

'He knows now,' he said, 'because I've told him.'

'He knew all the time,' said the other. 'I wonder what dirt he has in store for you.'

He thought a moment. That active brain which had foreseen the drought of '04 and banked on the cotton famine of '08 was very busy.

'What is he going to do?' he asked suddenly. 'What is the plan on which he is working? – I don't know, although I was in the syndicate: none of the others know. He has got the whole thing written out and deposited in the Jewel House. No eye but his has seen it.'

Leete rose to change into his street clothes.

'We could smash Kerry if we knew,' continued Zeberlieff thoughtfully. 'I'd give a million dollars to know what his plans are.'

Whilst Leete dressed, the other sat with his chin on his clenched fists, frowning at the street below. Now and again he would change his position to make a note.

When Leete returned, ready for an interview which he had arranged with King Kerry, Zeberlieff was almost cheerful.

'Don't go till Gleber comes,' he said. And Mr Leete looked at his watch regretfully. Before he could excuse himself, the servant announced the man for whom Zeberlieff was waiting.

Gleber proved to be a little colourless man, with a very bald head and a manner which was birdlike and mysterious.

'Well?'

'The young lady came at ten o'clock,' he said. 'She stood outside the office for ten minutes, then went in.'

'The same girl that lunched at the Savoy?' asked Zeberlieff, and the man nodded.

'That's the Marion girl,' said Leete with a grin. 'A bit of a shop-girl – is he that sort of fellow?'

Zeberlieff shook his head with a frown.

'He's a pretty good judge. How long did she stay?' he asked the man.

'She hadn't come out when I left. I think she's permanent there.'

'Rot!' snapped Leete. 'What is he going to keep a girl in his office for – a girl of that class?'

Still Zeberlieff indicated that he did not accept the other's view.

'This is the perfect secretary he has always been chasing,' he said. 'That girl is going to be a factor, Leete – perhaps she is already.' He bit his forefinger reflectively. 'If she knew!' he said half to himself.

Leete took a hurried farewell, and reached the office of the Big Trust a few minutes after time.

King Kerry was there, and Miss Marion was also there, seated at a rosewood desk behind a pile of papers with every indication of permanency.

'Sit down, Mr Leete,' invited Kerry with a nod, as his visitor was announced. 'Now, exactly what is your proposition?'

Mr Leete glanced significantly at Elsie, and the girl half rose. A movement of Kerry's hand checked her.

'I have no business secrets from Miss Marion,' he said.

Mr Leete's irascible bosom glowed with wrath. That he, a magnate by all standards, should be obliged to speak openly before a shop-girl – even an ex-shop-girl – was galling to his proud spirit.

'There's not much to say,' he said with an assumption of care-lessness which he was far from feeling. 'I've told you in my letter, that I am Goulding's, and I sell at a price.'

'You did not reveal the fact that you were the guiding spirit of Goulding's before I bought your other business,' said Kerry with a little smile. 'You were not even on the board – your solicitor acted for you, I presume?'

Mr Leete nodded.

'Of course, I knew all about it,' said King Kerry calmly. 'That is why I bought the cheaper property. What do you want for your precious store?'

'A million and a quarter,' replied Leete emphatically; 'and not a penny less.'

Kerry shook his head.

'Yours is a hand-to-mouth business,' he said slowly. 'You pay medium dividends and you have no reserves.'

'We made a profit of a hundred and fifty thousand last year,' responded Leete with a quiet smile.

'Exactly – a little over ten per cent of the price you ask – yet I offer you five hundred thousand pounds in cash for your business.'

Mr Leete got up from his chair very deliberately and pulled on his gloves.

'Your offer is ridiculous,' he said. And, indeed, he thought it was.

King Kerry rose with him.

'It is a little under what the property is worth,' he said; 'but I am allowing a margin to recoup me for the sum I gave for Tack and Brighten – the sum in excess of its value.'

He walked with the visitor to the door.

'I would ask you to come to lunch and talk it over,' he said; 'but, unfortunately, I have to go to Liverpool this afternoon.'

'All the talking-over in the world wouldn't alter my offer,' said Mr Leete grimly. 'Your proposition is absurd!'

'You'll be glad to take it before the year's out,' said King Kerry, and closed the door behind the inwardly raging Mr Leete.

He hailed a taxi, and arrived at his flat incoherent with wrath, and Hermann Zeberlieff listened with calm interest to a story calculated to bring tears to the eyes of any speculative financier.

That afternoon a young and cheerful reporter of *The Monitor*, prowling about Middlesex Street in search of copy, saw a familiar face disappear into the 'Am Tag', a frowsy club frequented by Continental gentlemen who described themselves variously as 'Social Democrats' and 'Anarchists', but who were undoubtedly expatriated criminals of a very high order of proficiency.

The enterprising reporter recognized the gentleman in spite of his poor dress, and followed him into the club with all the aplomb peculiar to the journalist who scents a good story.

CHAPTER VIII

Elsie Marion went back to her lodgings in Smith Street, Southwark, humming a little tune. It was incredible, yet here was the patent fact. She patted her little suede bag tenderly, and the crackle of stationery brought a happy little smile to her lips.

For in the bag was deposited that most wonderful of possessions – a contract. A contract drawn up in the most lucid phraseology which lawyers permit themselves, typed on a stiff sheet of paper inscribed with the tiny 'L' and an address which characterized the stationery of the Big Trust, in which she 'hereinafter called the employee of the one part', agreed to serve for the term of five years the president of the London Land Trust, 'hereinafter called the employers of the other part', for the sum of £780 per annum, payable weekly. .

Presently, she thought, she would wake up from her dream to the sordid realities of life spent amidst the bricks and mortar of mean streets, to the weary, hungry round of days divided between a high stool and a lumpy flock bed. Yet though her heart sang gaily at the new vistas opening for her, at the wondrous potentialities of her miraculously acquired wealth, something like a pang came to her at the thought of leaving Smith Street. The bed was lumpy, the breakfast served solidly, thick bread and butter on thick plates, and glutinous coffee in what she had christened Mrs Gritter's soundproof cups; the room, with its tiny bookshelves, its window-boxes, and its general neatness was redolent of much happiness. It was home to her – the only one of her own where she was mistress – that she had known.

Mrs Gritter's daughter was a trial certainly. Henrietta was a slatternly girl of twenty-four, mysteriously married and as mysteriously deserted – (the mystery was all Mrs Gritter's, for the neighbourhood knew the story). She was now a chronic inebriate, and the lodgers of 107, Smith Street were for ever meeting her in her most dazed condition, to the intense annoyance of Mrs Gritter, who was in the habit of saying that she did not mind Henrietta's weakness, but strongly condemned Henrietta's indiscretion in making it known.

But there were pleasant associations. Elsie had made friends amongst people who worked hard and lived decently on salaries which would scarcely suffice to pay for her Savoy lunch. As she was about to insert her key in the door of number 107, it opened and a young man stood in the entrance.

'Hullo, Miss Marion,' he said cheerily. 'You're home early tonight.'

Gordon Bray occupied the second floor front, and was something outside of the run of men she had met. He was a splendid specimen of the self-educated man who had triumphed over the disadvantages which a poverty-stricken upbringing and inadequate schooling had brought him. He had been denied even the opportunities for securing a scholarship through the council schools, for his association with the unbeautiful school in Latimer Road had ended abruptly when he found himself the sole support of a widowed mother at the age of fourteen. Errand boy, printers' devil, shop-boy, clerk – he had progressed till the death of his mother had shocked him to a realization of actualities. Tragic as that death had been, it had offered him a larger opportunity for advancing himself. His tiny income, which had sufficed for both, now offered a margin of surplus, and he had thrown himself into new fields of study.

There are thousands of Gordon Brays in the world: young men fighting bravely against almost insuperable odds. Handicapped by a lack of influence, they must fight for their own openings, and woe to them if they have no goal or, having one, deviate by one hairbreadth from the path they have set themselves.

The girl looked at him kindly. She was not in love with this good-looking boy, nor he with her. Between them existed a sympathy rarer than love. They were fellow-fighters in the big conflict of life, possessed common enemies, found similar inspirations.

'I'm off to the "Tec",' he said, and swung a bundle of books without shame. 'I'm getting so tired of Holdron's – they raised my salary by five shillings a week today and expected me to be overwhelmed with gratitude.'

She wanted to tell him her great news, but the fear that even a tiny spark of envy might be kindled in his heart stopped her. She would tell him another time when he was more cheerful.

'How are the models?' she asked. His goal was architecture, and those splendid models of his were the joy of his life. Moreover, they had material value, for he had won two gold medals at the school with a couple.

A momentary cloud passed over his face; then he grinned cheerfully.

'Oh, they're all right,' he said, and with a nod left her.

She ran up the stairs lightheartedly, passing on her way Mrs Gritter's disreputable daughter already far advanced in intoxication. Mrs Gritter brought the inevitable tea herself, and offered the inevitable comments on the weather and the inevitable apology for her daughter's condition.

'I'm going to leave you, Mrs Gritter,' said the girl.

'Oh, indeed?' Mrs Gritter felt such occasions called for an expression of injured innocence. She regarded 'notice' in the light of a censure upon her domestic capacities.

'I – I've got something better to do,' the girl went on; 'and I can afford a little more rent –'

'There's the first floor front, with foldin' doors,' suggested Mrs Gritter hopefully. 'If you could afford another ten shillings.'

The girl shook her head laughingly.

'Thank you, Mrs Gritter,' she said; 'but I want to live nearer my work –'

'Tube practically opposite the 'ouse,' persisted the landlady; buses to and fro, so to speak. It's very hard on me losin' two lodgers in a week.'

'Two?' asked the girl in surprise.

The landlady nodded.

'Between you and me and the gatepost,' she said confidentially and polishing her spectacles with the corner of her alpaca apron, 'Mr Bray has been a trial – always behind with his rent an' owes me three weeks.'

The girl was shocked. She had never troubled to enquire into the young man's affairs. She knew, of course, that he was not any too well off, but it never occurred to her that he was so desperately hard up. She understood now the bitterness in his voice when he spoke of his five shillings rise.

'It's studying that does it,' said Mrs Gritter mournfully; 'wastin' money on puttin' things in your head instead of puttin' 'em in your stummick an' on your back. What's the good of it? Education! It fills the prisons an' the workhouses and – and the army!'

She had a son in the army, and she bore the junior service a grudge in consequence; for sons in Southwark mean a contribution to the family finance.

The girl bit her lip in thought.

'Perhaps,' she hesitated. 'Perhaps if I were to pay you – the arrears?'

A gleam came into the landlady's eyes only to vanish again.

'That's no good,' she said. 'Besides, he's given me some things to hold for the money.'

'Some things?' Elsie looked at the woman from under her brows. 'What things?'

Mrs Gritter avoided her eyes.

'Not his models?' asked the girl quickly.

Mrs Gritter nodded.

'To 'ave and to 'old,' she said, mistakenly imagining she was indulging in legal terminology, 'until he doth pay.'

She had a passion for phrases of a certain sonorous type.

'You ought not to have allowed him to do so,' said the girl, stamping her foot. 'You knew that he would pay in time!'

Mrs Gritter sniffed.

'He didn't exactly give 'em to me,' she said; 'but I seized 'em according to lawr!'

The girl stared at her as though she were some strange new insect.

'You seized them?' she asked. 'Took them out of his room?'

Mrs Gritter nodded complacently.

'According to the lawr,' she justified herself.

'Why – why, you're not honest!' cried the girl.

A dull red rose to the cheeks of the excellent Mrs Gritter. 'Not honest!' she said, raising her voice to its full strident pitch. 'Don't you go saying things like that about respectable people, miss –'

There came a knock at the door, a sharp authoritative knock. Then, without waiting for permission to enter, the door opened and two men came in.

'Marion?' asked one.

'I am Miss Marion,' replied the girl, wondering what this unceremonious entry meant.

The man nodded in a friendly way.

'I am Sergeant Colestaff of the Metropolitan Police,' he said, 'and I shall take you into custody on a charge of stealing the sum of fourteen pounds, the property of your employers, Messrs Tack and Brighten.'

She did not faint.

She stood like a figure carved in stone, motionless.

Mrs Gritter eyed her darkly and muttered, 'Not honest!'

'Who charges me?' the girl asked faintly.

'Mr King Kerry,' said the detective.

'King Kerry – no, no!' Her hands went out and caught the detective's arm imploringly.

'It is Mr King Kerry,' he said gently. 'I am executing this warrant on information which he has sworn.'

'It's impossible – impossible!' she cried, her eyes filling with tears. 'It can't be – there must be a mistake! He couldn't do it – he wouldn't do it!'

The detective shook his head.

'There may be a mistake, Miss Marion,' he said gently; 'but what I have said is true.'

The girl sank into a chair and covered her face with her hands.

The detective's hand fell upon her shoulder. 'Come along, please,' he said. She rose, and, putting on her hat mechanically, went down the stairs with the two men, leaving the landlady speechless.

'Not honest!' she said at last. 'My gawd! What airs these shop-girls give theirselves!'

She waited till she heard the front door close, then she stooped to pull the girl's box from under the bed. If ever there was a time to pick up a few unexpected trifles it was now.

CHAPTER IX

Elsie Marion sat on the wooden bed and stared at the white-washed wall of her cell. She heard a church clock strike twelve. She had been six hours in custody; it seemed six years. She could not understand it.

King Kerry had parted from her cheerfully that afternoon to go to Liverpool to meet Cyrus Hatparl, newly arrived from America. She had accompanied the millionaire to the station and had stood chatting with him, taking his instructions for the work he wished her to do on the following day.

At Liverpool – so she had gathered from a sympathetic station inspector – he had sworn an affidavit before a justice of the peace, and at the telegraphed request of the Liverpool police a London magistrate had issued the warrant.

Why could he not have waited until he returned? She could have explained – whatever there was to be explained – but he was too impatient to shatter the little paradise which he so lately created. All through the evening she had sat wondering, racking her brains to think of some explanation for this terrible change in her fortunes. The thing was inexplicable – too vast a tragedy for her comprehension.

She had never handled large sums of money; accounts were made up daily, and they had never been questioned. There was another mystery. At eight o'clock that night her dinner had been sent in. It had been brought in a cab from the best hotel in London, the newly erected Sweizerhof; as perfect a meal as even an epicure could desire. She was young and healthy, and in spite of the seriousness of her position, she enjoyed the meal. As to why it came she could only elicit the information that it had been ordered by telephone from Liverpool by a gentleman.

The inconsistency of the man was amazing. He could cause her arrest for a charge of stealing a few pounds and could spend almost as much as she was supposed to have stolen on one meal.

One o'clock struck; she tried to sleep but could not.

At half-past one the wardress came down the corridor and unlocked her cell door.

'Come this way, miss,' she said, and the girl followed her through another steel-faced door, up a flight of steps to the charge room. She stopped dead as she entered the room, for standing by the inspector's desk was King Kerry.

He came towards her with outstretched hands. 'My poor child!' he said, and she could not doubt the genuineness of his concern. He led her to the desk. The girl was too dazed to resist.

'I think it is all right, inspector,' he said.

'Quite all right, sir,' said the officer, smiling at the girl. 'You are at liberty, miss.'

'But I don't understand,' she began. Then King Kerry took her arm and led her from the room.

Outside three cars were waiting and little groups stood on the sidewalk chatting. They turned as if at an order as the two came down the steps of the station, and one came up and raised his hat.

'I think, sir, we had better go to 107, Smith Street, first,' he said.

'I agree, superintendent,' said Kerry gravely.

He opened the door of the first car and lifted the girl in.

'My child,' he said when they were alone, 'you must suspend your judgement on me; none of my friends were in town. I had to take a drastic action, one which I was sure would not miscarry.'

'But, but – why?' she was crying, and her sobs went straight to the man's heart.

'Suspend your judgement,' he said gently. 'I believe that in arresting you I saved your life.'

He spoke so earnestly, so solemnly, that the tears ceased as a natural curiosity overcame her sense of grievance.

'I had a telegram on the train,' he said. 'I got it just as we were pulling into Liverpool – it must have come aboard at Edgehill. It was from my agent – a youngster on *The Monitor* – and was to the effect that for a reason which I understand and which, one of these days, you will understand, an attempt was to be made, tonight, on your life.'

'Impossible!'

He nodded.

'I could have informed the police, but I doubt whether they would have taken me seriously. I was terrified lest they protected you in some halfhearted way.'

'But who would want to harm me?' she asked. 'I haven't an enemy in the world.'

He nodded.

'You have as many enemies as any other member of society,' he said; 'that is to say, you have the enemies which are invariably opposed to the honest and decent members of society.'

He did not speak again until the car stopped before her lodging. The other cars were pulling up as she descended with her employer, and there was a brief consultation between Kerry and the detectives – for Scotland Yard and Pinkerton's men they were. Then King Kerry walked to the door of the dark and silent house and knocked a long, thundering roll.

He turned to the girl.

'Is your room in the front of the house?' he asked.

She shook her head smilingly.

'That has been far too expensive a situation,' she said. 'No, I have a room at the back on the first floor, with an excellent view of other people's back windows and a private promenade – if I had the courage to climb out.'

'A private promenade?'

He asked the question sharply, and she hastened to explain her facetious reference.

'I can step out of my window on to the leads,' she said. 'They form the roof of the kitchen. I rather like the idea because I am terrified of fire.'

'So am I,' said the multi-millionaire grimly.

The door opened as he spoke and Gordon Bray stood in the doorway fully dressed. He recognized Elsie immediately.

'Thank God, you have come!' he said. 'I've been worrying myself to death about you; I called at the station. I suppose they didn't tell you?' She introduced the millionaire, and the young man glanced curiously at her large escort.

'Mr Bray,' said Kerry, 'we want to arouse your landlady; can you do this for us?'

'Certainly.'

He led the way to the fusty little sitting room and lit the gas.

'Couldn't I?' asked the girl. 'I have to go up to my room.'

'Not yet, please,' answered Kerry quickly. 'Whatever happens, you are not to sleep in your room tonight. I have arranged a suite at the Sweizerhof, and I have already sent two ladies there to chaperon you,' he chuckled. 'You wouldn't think it was possible to get a chaperon in the middle of the night, would you?'

'No,' she smiled.

'Yet I got two,' he said. 'I telegraphed to the London Hospital and told them to send two of their nicest nurses – there was a chance that you might have collapsed and I knew that they would serve as guardians anyway. One thing more.'

He was very serious now.

'Yesterday I told you to remember three words – words I made you swear you would never reveal to any soul save me, or in the event of my death to my executors!'

She nodded. He had dropped his voice to a little above a whisper.

'You remember them?'

'Yes,' she replied in the same tone; 'the words were "Kingsway needs paving."'

He nodded. 'I asked you never even to use words!'

'I kept my promise,' said the girl quickly.

He smiled. 'You need not, any more,' he said. 'After tonight you may employ them as often as you like. I ought not to have told you.'

They were interrupted by the return of Bray.

'Mrs Gritter is on her way down,' he said. 'She isn't an elaborate dresser.'

King Kerry threw a swift glance at the young man, a glance which took him in from head to toe. He saw a fair-haired youth of twenty-two, with two honest blue eyes and as firm a chin as he himself possessed. The forehead was high and broad and the fingers which drummed noiselessly on the table were long and delicate.

It was said of King Kerry that he understood two things well – land and men, and in the general term 'men' was included woman in some of her aspects. He knew Gordon Bray from that moment of scrutiny, and never knew him better – as a man.

Mrs Gritter came blinking into the light; a shawl, a skirt, and a pair of slippers, plus an assortment of safety pins, being sufficient to veil her night attire. 'Hello!' she said, a little flustered by the sight of Kerry and not a little embarrassed by the unexpected spectacle of Elsie; 'thought you was safe for the night.'

Her humour was forced, and she was obviously uncomfortable.

'I wish to go to Miss Marion's room and collect some other things,' said Kerry to the girl's surprise.

Mrs Gritter was more embarrassed than ever, but it was not at the impropriety of a gentleman invading a lady's bedroom in the small hours of the morning.

'Oh,' she said a little blankly, 'that's awkward, my dear.'

She fixed a speculative and thoughtful eye upon Elsie.

'The fact is' – she cleared her throat with a little cough – 'the fact is, Miss Marion, I've taken a great liberty.' They waited. 'Ria happened to come in at ten minutes to eleven,' said the landlady apologetically, 'an' not feelin' well.'

Elsie concealed a smile. She had seen the lack-lustre eyes of Ria when she was 'not feeling well'.

'"Mother," she sez to me,' continued Mrs Gritter with relish, '"Mother," she sez, "you're not goin' to turn your only daughter into the street," she sez. "Well," I sez, "well, Ria, you know how I'm placed. There ain't a bed to spare except Miss Marion's, who's gone away to the country." I said that,' exclaimed Mrs Gritter, seeking approval, 'to keep the matter quiet.'

'In fact, your daughter is sleeping in Miss Marion's bed?' asked Kerry, and Elsie made a wry little face.

'And took the liberty of borrowin' Miss Marion's night-gown,' added Mrs Gritter, with a desire to get her sin off her mind.

Elsie laughed helplessly, but King Kerry was serious.

'Let us go in,' he said. 'You stay here, my child!'

Mrs Gritter walked to the door slowly.

'She's a heavy sleeper when she ain't well,' she said resentfully. 'What do you want to go up for?'

'I want to find out whether you are speaking the truth or not,' said Kerry, 'and whether it is your daughter or some other person occupying Miss Marion's room.'

'Oh, is that all?' asked Mrs Gritter, relieved; 'well, come up!'

She led the way, taking a lamp from the hall and lighting it. She paused outside the door of the first floor back.

'If Miss Marion misses anything from her box,' she said, 'it's nothing to do with me, or with my daughter.'

She turned the handle of the door and entered. Kerry followed. By the light of the lamp he saw a figure huddled beneath the bedclothes, and a tangle of disorderly hair spread on the pillow.

'Ria!' called Mrs Gritter loudly; 'Ria, wake up!' But the woman in the bed did not move.

Kerry passed the landlady swiftly, and laid the back of his hand on the pale cheek.

'I think you'd better go down,' he said gently, 'and tell the men you see outside the door I want them.'

'What do you mean?' asked the trembling landlady. He took the lamp from her shaking hand and put it on the chest of drawers.

'Your daughter is dead,' he said quietly. 'She has been murdered by somebody who came across the leads through that window.' He pointed to the window that was open.

King Kerry was speaking the truth in that solemn voice of his. She was dead, this poor, drunken soul, murdered by men who had come to force from Elsie's lips the words which would unfasten the combination lock on King Kerry's giant safe.

For Hermann Zeberlieff in his prescience had guessed right – King Kerry still locked his safe with the name of a street, and that street was 'Kingsway'.

CHAPTER X

It was a nine days' wonder, this murder of a drunken slut, and many were the theories which were advanced. The inquest proved that the woman had suffered from rough treatment at the hands of her assailants. She owed her death to strangulation.

No arrests were made, and the crime was added to the list of London's unravelled mysteries.

Four days after the sensational discovery, Elsie Marion sat behind her desk – an article of furniture which in itself was a pleasure to her – sorting over King Kerry's correspondence. Like many other great men, he was possessed of amiable weaknesses, and one of these was a disinclination to answer letters save those which were vital to his schemes. He recognized his own short-comings in this respect and the growing pile of letters, opened and unopened, produced a wince every time he had seen it.

Elsie had reduced the heap to something like a minimum. With the majority she found no occasion to consult her chief. They were begging letters, or the letters of cranks who offered wonderful inventions which would make their, and the exploiters', fortunes at small cost of time or money. There was a sprinkling of religious letters, too – texts heavily underlined admonishing or commending. Every post brought appeals from benevolent institutions.

In the drawer of her desk she had a chequebook which enabled her to draw money on an account which had been opened in her name. It was King Kerry's charity account, and she used her discretion as to the amount she should send, and the worthiness of the object. At first the responsibility had frightened her, but she had tackled her task courageously.

'It needs as much courage to sign a cheque as it does to starve,' was one of King Kerry's curious epigrams.

She worked splendidly through the pile of letters before her. Some went into the waste-paper basket; on some, after a knitting of brows and a biting of penholder, she scribbled a figure. She knew the people she was dealing with; she had lived amongst them, had eaten her frugal lunch at a marble-topped table across which professional begging-letter writers had compared notes unashamed.

She looked up as the commissionaire on duty came in with a card. She made a little grimace as she read the name.

'Does he know that Mr Kerry is out of town?' she asked.

'I told him, miss, but he particularly asked to see you,' said the man. She looked at the card again dubiously. It had its humorous side, this situation. A week ago, the perky Mr Tack never dreamt that he would be sending in his card to 'our Miss Marion' asking for an interview.

'Show him in, please – and, Carter –' as the man was at the door.

'Yes, miss?'

'I want you to stay in the room, please, whilst Mr Tack is here.'

The man touched his cap and went out, returning to usher in the late junior partner of Messrs Tack and Brighten.

He was all smiles and smirks, and offered his gloved hand with immense affability. 'Well, well!' he said in genial surprise, 'who'd have thought to see you in a comfortable situation like this!'

'Who, indeed!' she replied.

Uninvited he drew a chair up to the desk. 'You must admit that the training you had under me, and what I might term the corrective discipline – never harsh and always justified – has fitted you for this; now don't deny it!' He shook a finger playfully at her.

'It has certainly helped me to appreciate the change,' she said.

Mr Tack looked round at the waiting commissionaire, and then back to the girl with a meaning look.

'I'd like a few private words with you,' he said mysteriously.

'This is as private an interview as I can give you, Mr Tack,' said the girl with a smile. 'You see, I am not exactly a principal in the business, and I have neither the authority nor the desire to engage in any undertaking which is not also my employer's business.'

Mr Tack swallowed something in his throat, but inclined his head graciously.

'Very proper! very proper, indeed!' he agreed, with hollow cordiality. 'The more so since I hear rumours of a certain little trouble –' He looked at her archly.

The colour rose to her cheeks.

'There is no need to refer to that, Mr Tack,' she said coldly. 'Mr Kerry had me arrested because he knew that my life was in danger – he has given me fullest permission to tell why. When you go out you will see a steel safe in the front office – it has a combination lock which opened to the word 'Kingsway'. Mr Kerry gave me three words, the first of which would be the word which would open the safe. He told me this because he dare not write the word down. Then he realized that by doing so he had placed me in great danger. Men were sent to Smith Street, by somebody who guessed I knew the word, to force it from me, and Mr Kerry, guessing the plot, had me arrested, knowing that I should be safe in a police station. He came to London by special train to release me.'

She might have added that Kerry had spent three hours in London searching for the Home Secretary before he could secure an order of release, for it is easier to lock up than to unlock.

'Moreover,' she added, 'Mr Kerry generously offered me any sum I cared to mention to compensate me for the indignity.'

'What did you ask?' demanded Mr Tack eagerly, a contemptuous smile playing about his lips.

'Nothing,' she replied curtly, and waited for him to state his business.

Again he looked round at the solid commissionaire, but received no encouragement from the girl.

'Miss Marion,' he said, dropping his voice, 'you and I have always been good friends – I want you to help me now.'

She ignored the wilful misstatement of fact, and he went on. 'You know Mr Kerry's mind – you're the sort of young lady any gentleman would confide in: now tell me, as friend to friend, what is the highest Mr Kerry will give for Goulding's?'

'Are you in it, too?' she asked in surprise. She somehow never regarded him as sufficiently ingenious to be connected with the plot, but he nodded.

'The highest,' he repeated persuasively.

'Half a million,' said the girl. It was marvellous how easily the fat sum tripped from her lips.

'But, seriously?'

'Half a million, and the offer is open till Saturday,' she said. 'I have just written Goulding's a letter to that effect.'

'Oh dear! Oh dear! Oh dear! Oh dear!' said Mr Tack rapidly, but wearily. 'Why don't you persuade the old gentleman to be reasonable?'

A steely gleam came into her eyes. He remembered the episode of the inkpot and grew apprehensive.

'Which "old gentleman" are you referring to?' she asked icily.

Tack made haste to repair his error, and blundered still further. 'Of course,' he apologized, 'I oughtn't to speak like that about Mr Kerry.'

'Oh, Mr Kerry!' She smiled pityingly at the other. 'Mr Kerry is not, I should imagine, as old as you by ten years,' she said brutally. 'A strenuous life often brings grey hairs to a young man just as a sedentary life brings grossness to a middle-aged man.'

Mr Tack showed his teeth in a smile from which genuine merriment was noticeably absent.

'Ah, well,' he said, offering his hand, 'we mustn't quarrel – use your influence with Mr Kerry for good.'

'I hope I shall,' she said, 'though I cannot see how that is going to help you.'

He was in the street before he thought of a suitable response.

Oxford Street, and especially the drapery and soft goods section of Oxford Street, was frankly puzzled by the situation as it stood between Goulding's Universal Store and Tack and Brighten. It was recognized that Tack's – as it was called in drapery circles – could not fight against the rush and hustle of its powerful neighbour. Apparently King Kerry was doing nothing wonderful in the shape of resuscitating the business. He had discharged some of the old overseers, and had appointed a new manager, but there was nothing to show that he was going to put up a fight against his rival, who surrounded him literally and figuratively.

Goulding's offer had leaked out, and experts' view placed it as being exactly thirty-three per cent more than the business was worth; but what was Kerry to do?

Kerry was content apparently to flit from one department of trade to another. He bought in one week Tabards, the famous confectioner, the Regent Treweller Company's business, and Transome's, the famous Transome, whose art fabrics were the wonder and the joy of the world.

'What's his game?' asked the West End, and finding no game comprehensible to its own views, or measurable by its own standard, the West End decided that King Kerry was riding for a fall. Some say that the ground landlords had been taken into the Big Buyers' confidence; but this is very doubtful. The Duke of Pallan, in his recently published autobiography, certainly does make a passing reference to the matter which might be so construed; but it is not very definite. His Grace says –

'The question of selling my land in the neighbourhood of Regency, Colemarker, and Tollorton Streets was satisfactorily settled by arrangement with my friend Mr King Kerry. I felt it a duty in these days of predatory and pernicious electioneering...'

The remainder is purely political, but it does point to the fact that whether King Kerry bought the land, or came to a working arrangement with the ground landlords, he was certainly at one time in negotiation for their purchase. No effort was spared by those interested to discover exactly the extent of the 'L Trust's' aspirations.

Elsie, returning to her Chelsea flat one night, was met by a well-dressed stranger who, without any preliminary, offered her £5,000 for information as to the Trust's intended purchases. Her first impulse was to walk on, her second to be very angry. Her third and final resolution was to answer.

'You must tell your employer that it is useless to offer me money, because I have no knowledge whatever concerning Mr King Kerry's intentions.'

She went on, very annoyed, thereby obeying all her impulses together.

She told the millionaire of the attempt the next morning, and he nodded cheerily. 'The man's name was Gelber; he is a private detective in the employ of a Hermann Zeberlieff, and he will not bother you again,' he said.

'How do you know?' she asked in surprise.

He was always surprising her with odd pieces of information. It was a stock joke of his that he knew what his enemies had for dinner, but could never remember where he put his gloves.

'You never go home without an escort,' he said. 'One of my men was watching you.'

She was silent for a moment, then she asked, 'Does Zeberlieff dislike you?'

He nodded slowly. Into his face crept a look of infinite weariness.

'He hates me,' he said softly, 'and I hate him like the devil.'

She looked across at him and met his eyes. Was it over a question of business that their quarrel arose? As clear as though she had put the question in so many words, he read the unspoken query and shook his head. 'I hate him' – he hesitated – 'because he behaved badly to – a woman.'

It seemed that an icy hand closed over Elsie's heart, and for a few seconds she could hardly breathe. She felt the colour leave her face, and the room appeared blurred and indistinct.

She lowered her face, and fingered the letters on the desk before her. 'Indeed?' she said politely. 'That was – that was horrid of him!'

She heard the telephone bell ring, and he took up the receiver.

He exchanged a few words, then – 'I shall be back shortly,' he said. 'Mr Grant wants to see me.'

She nodded. Presently the door closed behind him with a click, and she dropped her head in her arms upon the table and burst into a passion of weeping. Love had indeed come into the life of Elsie Marion. It had all come upon her unawares, and with its light had brought its shadow of sorrow.

CHAPTER XI

'Where are you going tonight, Vera?'

Hermann Zeberlieff addressed the girl who stood by the window with a touch of asperity. The girl was standing by the window looking out across Park Lane to the Park itself. A cigarette glowed between her lips, and the soft, grey eyes were fixed far beyond the limit of human vision. She turned with a start to her half-brother and raised her dainty eyebrows as he repeated the question.

A simple gown of black velvet showed this slim, beautiful girl to the best advantage. The delicate pallor of the face contrasted oddly with the full, red lips. The shapely throat was uncovered in the fashion of the moment, and the neck of the bodice cut down to a blunt V, showed the patch of pure white bosom.

'Where am I going tonight?' she repeated; 'why, that's a strange question, Hermann – you aren't usually interested in my comings and goings.'

'I'm expecting some men tonight,' he said carelessly. 'You know some of them – Leete is one.'

She gave a little shudder.

'A most unwholesome person,' she said. 'Really, Hermann, you have the most wonderful collection of bric-a-brac in the shape of friends I have ever known. They are positively futurist.'

He scowled up at her. In many ways he was afraid of this girl, with her rich, drawling, southern voice. She had a trick of piercing the armour of his indifference, touching the raw places of his self-esteem. They had never been good friends, and only the provision of his father's will had kept them together so long. Old Frederick Zeberlieff had left his fortune in two portions.

The first half was to be divided equally between his son – the child of his dead wife – and the girl, whose mother had only survived her arrival in the world by a few hours.

The second portion was to be again divided equally between the two, 'providing they shall live together for a period of five years following my death, neither of them to marry during that period. For,' the will concluded, 'it is my desire that they shall know each other better, and that the bad feeling which has existed between them shall be dissipated by a mutual understanding of each other's qualities.' There were also other provisions.

The girl was thinking of the will as she walked across to the fireplace, and flicked the ash off her cigarette upon the marble hearth. 'Our menage as it is constituted ends next month,' she said, and he nodded.

'I shall be glad to get the money,' he confessed, 'and not particularly sorry to –'

'To see the end of me,' she finished the sentence. 'In that, at least, we find a subject upon which we are mutually agreed.'

He did not speak. He always came out worst in these encounters, and she puffed away in thoughtful silence.

'I am going to the Technical College to a distribution of prizes,' she said, and waited for the inevitable sarcasm.

'The Southwood Institute?' She nodded. 'You are getting to be quite a person in the charitable world,' he said, with a sneer. 'I shall never be surprised to learn that you have become a nun.'

'I know somebody who will!' she said.

'Who?' he asked quickly.

'Me,' said the girl coolly.

He sank back again in his chair with a growl.

'It is hard lines on you – my not getting married,' she went on. 'You get the whole of the inheritance if I do – during the period of probation.'

'I don't want you to marry,' he snarled.

She smiled behind the hand that held the cigarette to her lips. 'Poor soul!' she mocked; then, more seriously: 'Hermann, people are saying rather horrid things about you just now.'

He stared up at her coldly. 'What things, and what people?' he asked.

'Oh, paper people and the sort of bounder person one meets. They say you were in some way associated with –'

She stopped and looked at him, and he met her gaze unflinchingly.

'Well?'

'With a rather ghastly murder in Southwark,' she said slowly.

'Rubbish!' he laughed. 'They would suspect the Archbishop of Canterbury – it is too preposterous.'

'I don't know about that,' said the girl. 'I'm positively afraid of you sometimes; you'd just do anything for money and power.'

'Like what?'

She shrugged her shoulders. 'Oh, murder and things like that,' she said vaguely. 'There is a lot of good Czech in our blood, Hermann; why, sometimes you exasperate me so that I could cheerfully kill you.'

He grinned a little uncomfortably. 'Keep your door locked,' he said, and his lips tightened as at an unpleasant thought.

'I do,' she replied promptly, 'and I always sleep with a little revolver under my pillow.'

He muttered something about childishness, and continued his study of the evening paper.

'You see,' she went on thoughtfully, 'it would make an awful big difference to you, Hermann, if I died suddenly from ptomaine poisoning – or whatever weird diseases people die from – or if I walked in my sleep and fell out of a window.'

'Don't say such beastly things!' he snapped.

'It would make you richer by seven million dollars – recoup all your losses, and place you in a position where you could go on fighting that nice grey man – King Kerry.'

He got up from his chair; there was a ghost of a smile on his face.

'If you're going to talk nonsense, I'm going,' he said. 'You ought to get married; you're getting vixenish.'

She laughed, throwing her head back in an ecstasy of enjoyment.

'Why don't you pick up one of your tame students?' he sneered. 'Marry him – you'll be able to do it in a month – and make him happy. You could teach him to sound his h's with a little trouble.'

She had stopped laughing, and was eyeing him as he stood with the edge of the open door in his hand.

'You've a merry wit,' she said. 'Poor Daddy never realized it as well as I. There's a coarse fibre in the maternal ancestry of your line, Hermann.'

'You leave my mother's relations alone!' he said in a burst of anger.

'God knows I do,' she said piously. 'If various United States marshals and diverse grand juries had also left them alone, many of them would have died natural deaths.'

He slammed the door behind him before she had concluded her sentence. The mocking smile passed from her face as the door closed, and in its place came a troubled frown. She threw away the end of her cigarette and crossed the room to a small writing-table between the two big windows.

She sat for some time, a pen in her hand and a sheet of paper before her, undecided. If she wrote she would be acting disloyally to her half-brother – yet she owed him no loyalty. Behind her drawling contempt was an ever-present fear, a fear which sometimes amounted to a terror. Not once, but many times in the last year, she had intercepted a glance of his, a look so cold and speculative, and having in it a design so baleful that it had frozen her soul with horror. She thought of the insidious attempts he had made to get her married. The men he had thrown in her way, the almost compromising situations he had forced upon her with every variety of man from college youth to middle-aged man about town.

If she were married she were dead so far as the inheritance went – if she were not married by the thirtieth of the month, would she still be alive?

There was, as she knew, a streak of madness on Hermann's side of the family. His mother had died in an insane asylum. Two of her blood relations had died violently at the hands of the law, and a cousin had horrified San Francisco with a scene of murder of a peculiarly brutal character.

She had reason to believe that Hermann himself had been mixed up in some particularly disgraceful episode in New York, and that only on the payment of huge sums amounting to hundreds of thousands of dollars the victim and her relations had staved off an exposure. Then there was the case of Sadie Mars, the beautiful young daughter of a Boston banker. No money could have hushed that up – but here family pride and the position of the girl's parents saved Hermann. He went abroad, and the girl had taken an overdose of chloral with fatal results.

Wherever he went, disaster followed; whatever he touched, he made rotten and bad; he lifted the wine of life to the lips of the innocent, and it was vinegar and gall. She thought all this, and then she began to write rapidly, covering sheet after sheet with her fine calligraphy. She finished at last, enclosed her letter in an envelope, and addressed it. She heard his footstep in the hall without, and hastily thrust the letter into her bosom.

He looked across at the writing-table as he entered.

'Writing?' he asked.

'Doing a few polite chores,' she answered.

'Shall I post them for you?'

He made a show of politeness.

'No, thank you!' said the girl. 'They can be posted in the ordinary way – Martin can take them.'

'Martin is out,' he said.

She walked quickly to the bell and pushed it. Hermann looked at her strangely.

'There's no use ringing,' he said. 'I have sent Martin and Dennis out with messages.'

She checked the inclination to panic which arose in her bosom. Her heart was beating wildly. Instinct told her that she stood in deadly peril of this man with the sinister glint in his eyes.

'Give me that letter!' he said suddenly.

'Which letter?'

'The letter you have been writing so industriously for the last ten minutes,' he said.

A scornful smile curved her lips. 'Not the keyhole, Hermann!' she protested with mock pain. 'Surely not the keyhole – the servants' entrance to domestic secrets!'

'Give me that letter!' he said roughly.

She had edged away and backward till she stood near one of the big French windows. It was ajar, for the evening had been close. With a sudden movement she turned, flung open the long glass door, and stepped out on to the tiny balcony.

He went livid with rage, and took two quick steps towards her, then stopped. She was addressing somebody.

'Oh, I'm so sorry, Mr Bray; have you been ringing long?' An indistinct voice answered her. 'My brother will let you in; thank you so much for calling for me.'

She turned to Hermann Zeberlieff.

'Would you mind opening the door to one of my "tame students"? You will find he sounds his h's quite nicely!' she said sweetly.

'Damn you!' snarled the man, but obeyed.

CHAPTER XII

'Will you entertain Mr Bray whilst I get ready to go out?'

Hermann muttered his sulky compliance. He would have liked to refuse point blank, to have indulged himself in a display of temper, if only to embarrass the girl; but he had sufficient command of himself to check his natural desire. He scowled at the young man with whom he was left alone, and answered in monosyllables the polite observations which Gordon Bray offered upon men and things. There was no evidence in either the attire or in the speech of the technical student to suggest that he was of any other class than that of the man who examined him so superciliously.

'I gather you're one of the people my sister is distributing prizes to,' said Hermann rudely.

'Not exactly,' said the other quietly. 'Miss Zeberlieff is very kindly giving the gold medal for drawing, but the Countess of Danbery is actually making the award.'

'It doesn't matter much who makes it so long as you get it,' answered Hermann, summarizing his philosophy of life in one pregnant sentence.

'As a matter of fact I am not even getting it,' said the other. 'I took this medal last year – it represents an intermediate stage of tuition.' Hermann walked up and down the room impatiently. Suddenly he turned to the visitor.

'What do you think of my sister?' he asked.

Gordon went red: the directness of the question flung at him at that moment caught him unawares. 'I think she is very charming,' he said frankly, 'and very generous. As you know, she interests herself in education and particularly in the schools.'

Zeberlieff sniffed. He had never set himself the task of keeping track of his sister's amusements except in so far as they affected his own future. His own future! He frowned at the thought. He had had heavy losses lately. His judgement had been at fault to an extraordinary degree. He had been caught in a recent financial flurry, and had been in some danger of going farther under than he had any desire to go. He had plenty of schemes – big schemes with millions at their end, but millions require millions. He had put a proposition to the girl, which she had instantly rejected, that on the day of the inheritance they should pool their interests, and that he should control the united fortunes.

If the truth be told, there was little to come to him. He had anticipated his share of the fortune, which was already half mortgaged. In twelve days' time Vera would be free to leave him – free to will her property wherever she wished. Much might happen in twelve days – the young man might also be very useful.

His manner suddenly changed. He was perfectly learned in the amenities of his class, and there were people who vowed that he was the ideal of what a gentleman should be. His sister was not amongst these.

'Why don't you sit down?' he asked, and took up the thread of technical education with the convincing touch of the dilettante who has all the jargon of science with little backing of knowledge. He kept the young man pleasantly engaged till Vera returned.

Her car was waiting at the door, and he assisted her to enter. 'My brother was very entertaining, I gather?' she said.

'Very.'

She glanced at him, reading his face.

'You are very enthusiastic,' she said mockingly.

He smiled. 'I don't think he knows much about architecture,' he said. He had the habit of wholesome frankness, appreciated here, however, by one who lived in an atmosphere which was neither candid nor wholesome.

He thought he had offended her, for she did not speak again till the car was running over Westminster Bridge. Then – 'You will meet my brother again,' she said. 'He will discover your address and invite you to lunch. Let me think.' She knitted her forehead. 'I am trying to remember what happened before – Oh, yes! he will invite you to lunch at his club, and encourage you to speak about me; and he will tell you that I am awfully fond of chocolates, and a couple of days afterwards you will receive a box of the most beautiful chocolates from an unknown benefactor, and, naturally, when you have recovered from your astonishment at the gift, you will send it along to me with a little note.'

Whatever astonishment such a happening might have had upon him, it could not exceed that which he now felt. 'What an extraordinary thing you should have said that!' he remarked.

'Why extraordinary?' she asked.

'Well,' he hesitated. 'As a matter of fact, he has already asked me my address, and he did mention not once, but twice, that you were awfully fond – not of chocolates, but of crystallized violets.'

She looked at him a little blankly. 'How crude!' was all she said then; but later she half turned on the seat of the limousine and faced him.

'When those violets arrive,' she said quietly, 'I want you to take the parcel just as it is – wrapping and string and postmark – to Mr King Kerry: he will understand.'

'King Kerry?'

'Don't you like him?' She asked quickly.

He hesitated. 'I think I do,' he replied, 'in spite of his some-what drastic methods.'

Elsie had told him the story of the arrest – indeed, King Kerry had half explained – and now he repeated the story of Elsie's peril.

The girl listened eagerly.

'What a perfectly splendid idea,' she said enthusiastically, 'and how like King Kerry!'

After the distribution, the speechmaking, the votes of thanks, and the impromptu concert which followed the function, the girl sought Bray out, the centre of a group of his fellow-students, who were offering their congratulations, for many prizes had come his way.

'I want you to take me home!' she said.

She was a lovely and a radiant figure in her long grey silk coat and her tiny beaver hat; but he saw with tender solicitude that she looked tired, and there were faint shadows under her eyes.

They had reached a point in their friendship where they could afford to be silent in one another's society. To him she was a dream woman, something aloof and wonderful, in the world, but not of it – a beautiful fragile thing that filled his thoughts day and night. He was not a fool, but he was a man. He could not hope, but he could – and did – love. From the day she came into his life, an interested – and perhaps amused – visitor to the schools, his outlook had changed. She was very worshipful, inspiring all that is beautiful in the love of youth, all that is pure and tender and self-sacrificing.

She was, he knew, very wealthy; he dreamt no dreams of miracles, yet he did not regard her money as being an obstacle.

It was she, the atmosphere which surrounded her, that held him adoring but passive.

'I want you to do something for me,' she said.

'I will do anything.'

There was no emphasis, no fervour in his voice, yet there was something in the very simplicity of the declaration which brought the colour to her cheek.

'I am sure you would,' she answered almost impulsively; 'but this is something which you may find distasteful. I want you to meet me in Regent Street tomorrow evening,' she said. 'I – I am rather a coward, and I am afraid of people –'

She did not finish the sentence, and offered no further elucidation to the mystery of a meeting which, so far from being distasteful, set the young man's heart aflutter afresh.

'At nine o'clock, at the corner of Vigo Street,' she said, when she left him, at the door of the Park Lane house, 'and you will have to be very obedient and very patient.'

She offered her hand, and he took it. She raised it higher and higher, and for a moment he did not understand. Then he bent and kissed it.

She had taken off her glove in the car with that idea.

CHAPTER XIII

King Kerry reread a letter which had arrived by the morning post, and, contrary to his custom, placed it in the inside pocket of his coat. His secretary watched the proceedings with apprehension, as marking a return to the bad old days; but he smiled and shook his head. He had a habit of reading her thoughts which was at once uncanny and embarrassing.

'This is a "really" letter,' he said, referring to a passage at arms they had had whether a letter was 'really private' or just 'private' – she had opened a score bearing the latter inscription, only to find that they were of the really begging-letter variety. Henceforth he passed the private letters under review, and judged only by the handwriting or the crest whether it was a confidential communication within the meaning of the Act.

Kerry sat for a long time at his desk, thinking; then, by and by, he took out the letter again and reread it. Whatever were its contents, they worried him, and presently he called a number on the phone which she recognized as being a firm of detectives allied to Pinkerton's. 'Send a man to me for instructions!' he said, and hung up the receiver.

For a long time he was writing furiously, and when the detective was announced, he had still a few more pages to write. He finished at last and handed the papers to the waiting man. 'This paper is to be carefully read, digested, and destroyed,' he said. 'The instructions are to be carried out without reservation, and you are to tell your chief to draw upon me to any extent in the execution of my orders.'

When the man had gone, he turned to the girl. 'It is a very hard world for women,' he said sadly, and that was all the reference he made to the letter or its sequel.

On the wall of the office hung a remarkable map. It was a large scale map of London, which had been especially prepared for 'The King' (the Press called him ironically 'The King of London'). Scarcely a day passed but an employee of the maker called to mark some little square, representing a shop or house, with green watercolour paint, King Kerry standing by and directing precisely where the colour patches were to be placed. The green was growing in the map. The Trust was buying up land and house property north, south, and west. Baling, Forest Hill, Brockley and Greenwich were almost all green. Kennington, Southwark, Wandsworth, Brixton, Clapham, and Tooting were well patched; but the object of the Trust was, apparently, to put a green belt around a centre represented by a spot midway between Oxford Circus and Piccadilly. Inside this circle, representing a mile radius, lay the immediate problem of the Trust.

The girl was looking across at the map, noting that the three new green patches which had been added that morning were almost dry, when she caught King Kerry's amused eyes fixed upon her. 'How would you like to pay a visit to the scene of your servitude?' he asked good-humouredly.

'Tack's?' she asked in wonder.

He nodded.

'I don't know,' she demurred. 'I should feel rather shy, I think.'

'You must get over that,' he said cheerfully. 'Besides, you will find very few people in the same positions in which you left them.'

A few moments later the car came round, and she took her place by his side.

'People are asking what I am going to do,' he said, as if reading her thoughts, 'and this old town is just shaking its hoary head at me. Tack's sold a hundred thousand pounds' worth of goods last year – they will sell half a million pounds' worth next year.'

She smiled, as at a good joke.

'You doubt it?' he asked, with a suggestion of that affectionate amusement which so often sent the colour to her cheeks.

'Do you know anything about a drapery store?' she asked, answering one question with another.

He shook his head; the word 'drapery' puzzled him.

'Drapery? – we call them soft goods,' he said. 'No, I know no more than I know about boots or railway trucks. People who learn in compartments – there are hundreds of proud fathers who boast their sons are learning their business from office boy to manager; but my opinion is that they usually pass their true vocation halfway between top and bottom. You needn't start life as a junior clerk to discover that you're an excellent salesman, and because you're an excellent salesman you needn't necessarily be a heaven-born president – you call them managing directors.'

She loved to listen to him when he was in this mood. It was a pity that Tack's was so near, but a block in the Regent Street traffic gave him time to expound his philosophy of business. 'The man who watches the window to see the articles that are sold will learn a lot if he has patience and plenty of time; but he will get cold feet. You've got to go to the manufacturing end to judge sales, and you have got to go to the man who pulls money out of manufacturing to learn that Mrs So-and-So prefers four buttons on her kid gloves to three. It all comes back to the money behind the manufacturer. There are very few bank managers in Manchester who did not know when beads ceased to be a fashionable attire in the Fiji Islands.'

He went back to Tack's and its future.

'Half a million pounds' worth of goods!' he laughed quietly, 'and all to be sold in a year at a little store that never had a bigger turnover than a hundred thousand – it means selling sixteen hundred pounds' worth of goods a day; it means many other things. My child, you are going to witness some sale!'

She laughed in sheer glee.

There was a considerable change in the appearance of Tack's even in the short space of time she had been away. The building was a fairly modern one. King Kerry was already reshaping it, and a small army of workmen was engaged day and night in effecting alterations which he had planned.

There had been a tiny little 'annexe', too small to dignify with the name. It had owed its existence to the discovery, after the building had been erected, that a piece of land, some twenty feet by twenty, which had been used by Goulding's as a temporary dumping ground for old packing-cases, and for some extraordinary reason had not been built upon, was part of this freehold. Mr Leete had run up a tiny building on the site (this was before he had acquired a controlling interest in Goulding's), and the place had been used as auxiliary storerooms. Workmen were engaged in removing the floors from the roof to the ground.

'I am having two large lifts put in there,' explained Kerry. 'They will be about the same size as tube lifts, only they will be much faster.'

Tack had always set his face against the elevator system, adopting the viewpoint that, as it was, people did not get sufficient exercise, and that he had no intention of encouraging laziness.

'But won't they be very large?' asked the girl. 'I mean too large?'

Kerry shook his head. 'Sixteen hundred pounds a day means about sixteen thousand purchasers a day, or a little under a thousand an hour.'

She thought she detected a flaw in his arithmetic, but did not correct him; he was surely calculating upon a twenty-four hour day!

Other re-arrangements included new dressing-rooms on the roof. Some of the counters had been taken away, and the broad window spaces upon which so much depended in the old days had been reduced by seventy-five per cent and the additional space afforded had been utilized for the erection of large flat trays. In place of the old window display, electricians were fitting long, endless belts of black velvet running the whole width of each window, upon which the lighter goods were to be displayed.

'Each article will have a big number attached and the price in plain figures: there will be a sample-room on the ground floor, where all the customer has to do is to ask to see the number she wants to purchase. When she has decided what she wants, she goes upstairs to the first floor and it is handed to her ready wrapped. There will be no waiting. Every sample clerk will have a little phone in front of her. She will be in constant communication with the packing-room. She will signal the purchases, and the customer has only to go to the counter, or one of the counters, bearing her initial, mention her name, and take the parcel.'

The girl looked at him in amazement. It seemed remarkable to her that he had thought all this out and that she was unaware of the fact.

'You are preparing for a rush?' she asked, and she said it in such a tone that he laughed.

'You don't think we shall be so busy, eh? Well, *nous verrons!*'

Elsie caught many envious glances cast in her direction. Old acquaintances have a trick of remembering friendships which never existed – especially with those who have been fortunate in life. She had had no close friends in the business, but there were many who now regarded her as a sometime bosom confidante, and were prepared to harbour a grievance against her if she did not hold them in like regard. Some called her 'Elsie', who had never before taken that liberty, doubtless with the desire to establish their intimacy before she advanced too far along the golden road. This is the way of the world. But Elsie was too warm-hearted to be cynical, and responded readily to their overtures of friendship.

Their salaries had been substantially raised, so 'Fluff', a pretty little girl in the 'White' department, told her. 'All the rotters have been sacked, three of the shop-walkers, and the manager of the "ready-mades",' said the girl enthusiastically. 'Oh, Miss Marion, it was splendid to see that beast Tack walk out for the last time.'

'Things are awfully comfortable,' said another – Elsie had an opportunity for gossiping whilst King Kerry interviewed the new manager – 'but there is going to be an awful rush, and those awful fines have been abolished. Oh! and they're taking on an awful number of girls, though where they're going to put 'em all heaven knows – we shall be awfully crowded!'

The girl bore the nickname of 'Awful Agnes', not without reason.

King Kerry rejoined Elsie, and they drove back to the office together. 'Had to take a big warehouse to stock our goods,' he explained. 'We shall sell a few! Every other shop in the street for two hundred yards in each direction is engaged in the same business as us. I have offered to buy the lot, but I guess they've got an exaggerated idea of the value of things.'

Whether they had or not, there were some who were prepared to fight the 'Big L'.

That same night there appeared in all the London evening papers the announcement that 'The Federal Trades of London' had been incorporated as a limited company. The list of the firms in the new combine included every store in Oxford Street engaged in the same business as Tack and Brighten's.

'The object of the Federation' (said the announcement) 'is to afford mutual protection against unfair competition. Each firm concerned will act independently so far as its finances are concerned, and the shareholders' interests will remain undisturbed. By means of this combine it is hoped that the pernicious operations of a certain American Trust will be successfully checked.'

The list of directors included Hermann Zeberlieff, Esq. (independent gentleman), and John Leete (managing director of Goulding's, Limited).

'Pernicious operations!' repeated King Kerry. 'Say, this paper doesn't like us!' He turned over the sheets of the *Evening Herald*. 'A bright little paper,' he mused. Then he took out his cheque book and signed his name in the bottom right-hand corner.

He blotted the signature, and passed the slip across to the girl.

'Elsie,' he said, and the girl flushed, for he had never before called her by her first name. 'The *Evening Herald* is on the market. They want sixty thousand pounds for the concern; they may take less. Here's a blank cheque. Go down and buy that durned paper.'

'Buy?' the girl gasped. 'I – but I don't – I can't – I'm not a business woman!'

'It's for sale – go and buy it; tell them you're King Kerry's partner.' He smiled encouragingly and laid his hand on hers. 'My partner,' he said softly. 'My dear little partner!'

CHAPTER XIV

Four men had been invited to dinner at 410, Park Lane, but only three had so far arrived. Worse than that, Vera, whom Hermann had particularly asked to grace the board with her presence, had pleaded the usual headache and had most emphatically refused to come down.

'You are trying to make me look a fool before these people,' he stormed. He interviewed her in her little den, and she was palpably unprepared for social functions of any description, being in her dressing-gown.

'My dear Hermann,' she said, 'don't rave! I have a headache – it is a woman's privilege.'

'You always have headaches when I want you,' he said sulkily.

She did not look any too well. He wondered –

'No,' she answered his unspoken thought. 'I noticed that the gas was turned on at the stove and off at the main, so I just turned it off at the stove, too.'

'What do you mean?' he asked roughly.

She smiled.

'I have always appreciated your gift – a stove in Sèvres ware must have cost a lot of money. When I lay down this afternoon the main was turned off – that I'll swear. When I woke up, it was on, though why anybody should turn on the gas on a warm July afternoon, I can't think.'

'Martin –' he began.

'Martin didn't touch it,' she said. 'I have asked him. Fortunately, no harm was done, because I had noticed the little tap was turned before I began to sleep. I am getting frightened, Hermann.'

His face was ghastly pale, but he forced a smile.

'Frightened, Vera – why?' he asked in his friendliest tone.

She shook her head at him slowly, her eyes never leaving his face.

'It is getting so near the time,' she said, 'and I feel somehow that I cannot bear up against the strain of always fighting for my life.'

'Rubbish!' he cried genially. 'Come along and see my people. Leete is one, Hubbard, one of the Federation directors, is another. Bolscombe hasn't turned up. Why don't you get rid of the worry of your money?' he said with a show of solicitude. 'Pool it with mine, as I suggested months ago. You'll go mad if you don't.' He stopped short and eyed her curiously. 'I think you're a little mad now,' he said slowly, and she shook her distress off and laughed.

'Hermann, you're the most versatile man I know,' she said; 'but so horribly unoriginal.'

'Are you going out tonight?'

He paused at the door to ask the question, and she nodded.

'With your headache?' he sneered.

'To get rid of it,' she replied.

He went downstairs to his guests.

'My sister is not very well,' he said. 'She's rather depressed lately – ?'

Then occurred the devilish idea: that flash of inspiration to villainy which has sent men to the gallows and has tenanted Broadmoor with horrible gibing things that once were human. Ten days! said the brain of Hermann Zeberlieff. Do it now!

With scarcely a pause he went on –

'We're all friends here, and I don't mind telling you that she is worrying me – she has distinctly suicidal tendencies.'

There was a murmur of commiseration.

'I'll just see how she is,' he said; 'and then we'll start dinner.'

'I thought I saw your sister standing at her window,' said Leete, and added with a smirk: 'I rather flattered myself that she was waving her hand to me.'

Hermann looked at him in frank surprise. He knew that Vera hated Leete as intensely as a woman with fine instincts could hate a man. It would be an unsuspected weakness in her if she endeavoured to make friends with his associates; but it bore out all that the girl had said. She was frightened, was clutching at straws, even so unsavoury a straw as Leete.

He walked carelessly from the room and mounted the stairs. He had in his heart neither fear nor remorse for the dreadful deed he contemplated. He did not go straight to where she was, but slipped into her bedroom, which communicated with the sitting room.

He stepped stealthily, silently.

By the side of the window was a long curtain-cord of silk. He drew a chair, stepped noiselessly upon it and severed the cord high up. He stepped down as noiselessly. He had three minutes to do the work. In three minutes' time he would be with his guests smiling apologetically for his sister's absence, by what time this beautiful creature of 'suicidal tendencies' would be hanging limply from –

He looked round for a suitable hook and found a peg behind the door which bore his weight.

That would be the place. Rapidly he made a noose at one end of the rope and held it in his hand behind him.

He turned the handle of the door and walked into the dressing-room. She was sitting by the window and rose, startled.

'What were you doing in my room?' she demanded.

'Stealing your jewels,' he said with humour. But she was not appeased by his simulated playfulness.

'How dare you go into my room?' she cried. The fear of death was upon her, through her brain ran a criss-cross of plans for escape.

'I want to talk things over,' he said and reached out his hand to touch her. She shrank back.

'What have you got behind your back?' she asked in a terrified whisper.

He sprang at her, flinging one arm about her so that he pinioned both arms. Then she saw his design as his other hand rose to close over her mouth. The coils slipped down on his arm and he shifted his left hand up to silence her.

'Mercy!' she gasped.

He smiled in her face. He found the noose and slipped it over her head. Then –

'Kerry knows – Kerry knows!' said her muffled voice. 'I wrote to him. There is a detective watching this house day and night – ah!'

The loop had touched her neck.

'You wrote?'

'Told him – murder – me – I signal every half-hour – due in five minutes –'

Very gently he released her, laughing the while. He had moved her to where he could see through the window. A man stood with his back to the railings of the Park, smoking a short cigar. He was watching the house for the half-hour signal.

'You never thought I was such a good actor,' said Hermann with his set smile.

She staggered to the window and sank in a chair.

'I didn't frighten you, did I?' he asked with a certain resemblance of tenderness.

She was shaking from head to foot. 'Go out!' she said. 'Go away! I know your secret now!'

With a little shrug he left her, taking the silk cord with him, for that evidence was too damning to leave behind. She waited till she heard him speaking in the hall below, then she fled to her room and locked the door. With shaking hands she made her preparations. She dressed as quickly as she had dressed in her life and descended the stairs. In the hall she saw Martin, and paused. 'Get me a walking-stick – any one will do – quickly!'

The man went away and, returning with the ivory-headed cane of her brother, found her by the open door.

She looked at her watch. It wanted twenty minutes to nine.

A taxi-cab carried her to Vigo Street, and the nearer she came to the man who she knew loved her, and to the freedom which was ahead the higher rose her spirits.

Gordon Bray was waiting. She paid the cab and dismissed it. 'I knew you would be here!' she said impulsively, and took his arm. 'Gordon,' she said breathlessly – it is strange how two people that day had been thrilled by the utterance of a Christian name – 'you have known me for three years.'

'And twenty-five days, Miss Zeberlieff,' said the young man. 'I count the days.'

The eyes turned to him were bright with a light he had never seen.

'Call me Vera,' she said softly. 'Please don't think I'm bold – but I just want you to – you love me, don't you?'

The street lights went round and round in a giddy whirl before the man. 'I worship you!' he said hoarsely.

'Then bear with me for a little while,' she said tenderly; 'and if I do things which you do not approve – ?'

'You couldn't do that,' he said.

There in Regent Street, before all the hurrying world, shocked, amused or interested, according to its several temperaments, she raised her lips to his and he kissed her.

'Now,' she said, and thrust him away, her eyes dancing, 'show me the new shop that King Kerry bought.'

'This is it' – he pointed along the block – 'the art fabric people. It was in all the papers.'

She ran along the pavement till she came to the darkened windows of the store. Then, without a warning, she raised her stick and sent the ivory head smashing through the plate glass.

A policeman seized her.

'My God!' said Gordon Bray. 'Why did you do that?'

'Votes for Women!' cried Vera and laughed. She was laughing still when they took her away in a cab to Marlborough Street, and laughing the next morning when she was sentenced to three weeks in the second division.

King Kerry, sitting at the solicitors' table with Bray, was not unamused. In three weeks Vera would be entitled to her share of her father's fortune, and her brother's machinations would be in vain. She would come out of prison a free woman in every sense of the word.

As for Bray, though he watched that delicate figure anxiously, he understood. It would be three weeks of hell for him with only the memory of those fragrant lips to help him bear the parting.

CHAPTER XV

'I couldn't get back to the office last night,' said Elsie, 'and I tried to get you on the phone, but you weren't anywhere you ought to have been.' Her voice was a little reproachful, for she had really wanted to see him to communicate a wonderful piece of news.

'I suppose I wasn't,' admitted King Kerry, smoothing his grey hair. There was something almost childlike about the millionaire when he was penitent, and Elsie's heart was very tender to him in such moments as these.

'A young friend of mine smashed one of my windows in Regent Street,' he said in extenuation. 'Really, I'm never out of these infernal police stations,' he added ruefully.

'A suffragette?'

'I guess so,' nodded Kerry, biting off the end of a cigar. 'Anyway, she's gaoled!'

'Oh!' protested the girl in horror. 'You didn't allow her to go to gaol?'

'I surely did,' admitted King Kerry with his brightest smile, 'and instructed a lawyer to press for it.'

He saw the troubled look on the girl's face and waited.

'It isn't like you, somehow,' she said, with a note of reproach in her voice. 'You're so kind and so tender to people in trouble – I just hate the thought of you being anything else than what I think you are.'

'Everybody is different to what people think they are,' he said mournfully. 'I guess you've never read what some of the New York papers said about my big railroad combine. I thought not,' as she shook her head. 'One of these days I'll hunt up the cuttings for you, and you'll see how black it is possible for a man to be – and escape gaoling.'

'You'll not convince me,' she said with decision. 'I'm not even satisfied that you did what you said this morning.'

He nodded vigorously.

'Sure,' he said; 'but I might as well tell you right here that the lady was a friend of mine, and she was most anxious to go to gaol – and I was obliged to help her.'

'She is really a suffragette?'

King Kerry considered before he made a reply, drawing thoughtfully at his cigar.

'No, she isn't,' he said. 'She's had enough to make her. If I were she, I guess I'd burn the whole of Regent Street. You'll read about it in the papers, anyway,' he said.

She opened a drawer and took out a copy of the *Evening Herald*.

'Read about it in your own paper,' she said proudly, and handed him the early edition.

He whistled. 'I'd almost forgotten that,' he said. 'So you bought it!'

She nodded. She made a pretty picture standing there with her hands behind her back, her cheeks flushed and her lovely eyes bright with excitement. She stood like a child who had deserved commendation and was waiting expectantly for her due.

'What did you give?' he asked.

'Guess?' she countered.

'Sixty thousand?' he suggested.

She shook her head.

'Fifty?' with raised eyebrows.

Again she shook her head.

'I'll tell you the whole story,' she said. 'When I got to the office of the *Evening Herald* I found the staff had gone home, but the editor, the manager, and the proprietor were in the board room, and I found out afterwards that there had been a most unholy row.'

'There always is when those three gentlemen meet,' said King Kerry with knowledge. 'If the publisher had been there too, you would have been obliged to ring for the ambulance.'

'Well,' she went on with a smile, 'I sent in your name and was admitted at once.'

'Such is the magic of a name,' murmured the millionaire.

'They were awfully surprised to see me, and the proprietor, Mr Bolscombe, started to "my girl" me, but he didn't continue when I put it to him straight away that I had called to buy the paper.'

'Did he faint?' asked Kerry, anxiously.

She smiled.

'Not exactly; but he asked sixty thousand pounds, whereupon I did all the fainting necessary. The paper is a young one – you know that?' – King Kerry nodded – 'and is just on the point of paying –'

'That's the editor's view,' suggested Kerry, and the girl nodded.

'Especially if the policy was changed a little –'

'Do I hear the manager speaking?' asked Kerry, looking up at the ceiling.

'Yes – but on the other hand it may not, and there was a doubt as to whether it was wise to throw good money after bad.'

Kerry laughed uproariously for him.

'That is the proprietor,' he said. 'I know what he'd say because I've seen him once or twice.'

'So we talked and we talked, and the end of it was I got the paper for forty thousand pounds,' she said triumphantly.

He rose and patted her on the shoulder.

'Excellent, child!' he said. 'I shall put that in my red book.'

He had a locked ledger in which from time to time he made entries, the nature of which was unknown save to the writer.

'I've something else to say,' said the girl. 'After I'd given the cheque and got the receipt I went home, and Mr Bolscombe, who was dining with – you'll never guess whom?' she challenged.

'Hermann Zeberlieff – yes?' retorted Kerry. 'Go on!'

She was a little disappointed that her baby bomb had not so much as fizzed.

'I went back to my flat. Three hours later Mr Bolscombe called, though how he got the address –'

'From Zeberlieff.'

'Of course – how absurd of me to forget. He called and offered to buy back the paper for seventy thousand pounds!'

'Excellent!' laughed King Kerry.

'He wanted to say that it wasn't a proper sale, but I made him include all the considerations in the receipt – was I right?'

'Child,' said the admiring Kerry solemnly, 'I shall take you into partnership one of these days. What was the end?'

She handed him the receipt. She had something more to say.

'The editor is rather a clever young man,' she said, hesitatingly; 'and the manager seems pretty capable. I told them that you would make no immediate changes.'

'Right again,' said Kerry heartily. 'A new man isn't always the best man, and the old man isn't necessarily a fool. Never change for change's sake – except your dress.'

He stood by his desk meditatively.

'This deserves more than the ordinary recognition,' he said with mock solemnity. 'Nothing less than a dinner can celebrate our first joint victory over the enemy.'

She looked at him with laughing eyes too near to tears for her complete satisfaction. That she had pleased the 'grey man', as she called him in her heart, was enough.

She had seen two handsome men in the past twenty-four hours – she puzzled her head to remember who the other was.

But it had not been the type that this man represented, the healthy skin and the laughing eyes, and that masterful chin – and the other had most certainly not been the owner of the greyest hair she had ever seen in a young man. She wondered why he was so grey. She had often wished to ask him, but something which was not the fear of impertinence (they had progressed too far in friendship for that fear to weigh with her) had prevented her.

'Dinner at eight at the Sweizerhof,' he said; 'and if you feel incapable of coming without a chaperon, bring somebody nice.'

'I don't know anybody nice enough,' she smiled, 'so you must bear with me alone.'

She had a day's work before her, and she tackled it with an energy which the prospect of an evening's enjoyment increased. In the middle of the morning she stopped.

'I know!' she said suddenly.

He looked up.

'What do you know?'

'The name of the other man – I mean,' she said hastily, 'the man who came with Mr Bolscombe to the flat. It was Mr Martin Hubbard.'

'Oh!' he said dubiously, 'The Beauty?'

'Is that what they call him? I can understand it. He's good-looking in a way, but –' She hesitated.

'There are lots of "buts" about Martin,' said Kerry quietly. 'I met him in New York. He's some dollar chaser.'

He stared meditatively at the wall ahead of him.

'A man who marries for money,' he said, 'is like a dog that climbs a steeple for a bone. He gets his meal, but there isn't any comfortable place to sleep it off.'

He made no further reference to Martin, and was busy for the rest of the day.

For he was drafting the advertisement which was to shake the drapery world to its foundations.

CHAPTER XVI

'When a man with no great moral perceptions, with no sense of obligation to his conscience, his pride, or his humanity, finds himself thwarted of his heart's desire, his mind naturally turns to murder. Murder, indeed, is a natural instinct of man, as maternity is a natural instinct of woman. Thousands of years of civilization have called into being a super-instinct which is voluntary in application and is termed self-restraint. The wild waters of will have been directed through artificial courses, and woe to the errant stream that overleaps the bank and runs to its natural level.'

So wrote Hermann Zeberlieff in his diary two nights after the sentence of his sister. It embodied his philosophy, and was one of the most interesting articles of his creed and certainly one of the most coherent passages in the diary which was read in public on a subsequent occasion, Hermann Zeberlieff being unavoidably absent.

His worst enemies will not deny to this perverse man a certain literary quality or cavil at the description given to him by Simnizberg, the anthropologist of 'Immoral Visionary'.

He finished the entry and put away the book in its private and proper place. He glanced with a sneer at the little stack of letters he had answered. Everybody who knew him had written kindly, indulgently, or humorously of his sister's exploit. Little did they know how much that freak of hers had cost him. It might have cost him dearer had she not gone, but this he would never accept as a possibility.

He went to his room to dress. Checked as he was by his sister's action, he was in a sense relieved that the necessity for removing her had departed. She would make a will in prison – he did not doubt that. Cassman, her solicitor, had been sent for to Holloway for that purpose. His attitude of mind would have baffled the average psychologist, for now he had no feeling of resentment toward her. Frankly, he wanted her money, as, frankly, he had not abandoned hope of getting it. But the method must be more subtle – he had invited Martin Hubbard to dinner with that object on the night of the extraordinary behaviour of Vera.

'Bolscombe is a fool' – he had a trick of talking to himself, and he was dressing without the aid of a valet – 'to sell the paper to that swine!'

'That swine' was King Kerry, toward whom this strange man directed the full force of his implacable hatred. He wondered what use King Kerry would make of his new toy – it was a weapon which might be easily employed to harass Hermann. It would not be the first time that 'The King of London' had bought newspapers to harass him. He had finished dressing when a discreet knock came to the door.

'There is a man who wishes to see you, sir,' said the servant who entered at Hermann's invitation.

'What kind of man?'

The servant was at a loss to describe the visitor.

'Poorish – foreign,' he said.

Poorish and foreign! Hermann could not place the visitor.

'Tell him to come up.'

'Here, sir?'

'Here,' said the master sharply. 'Where do you think I want to see him?'

The man was used to these unreasonable outbursts and was undisturbed by them. He went away and came back with a little man, rather pallid of face, who wore a straggling, irregular beard and clothes of sufficient poverty to justify the 'poorish' and just enough eccentricity to make 'foreign' an accurate guess.

'Oh, it is you, is it?' said Hermann coolly. 'Sit down – you need not wait, Martin.'

'Well?' he asked when they were alone. 'What do you want?'

He spoke in French, and the little man raised his expressive hands deprecatingly.

'What else, *mon vieu* – but money? Ah, money is a horrible thing, but necessary.'

Hermann opened a gold cigarette case deliberately and selected a cigarette before he replied.

'Exactly why should you come to me?'

The little man shrugged his shoulders and glanced at the ceiling for inspiration. He was an unpleasant-looking man with a short, squat nose and small, twinkling eyes set wide apart. His skin was blotched and unhealthy, and his hands were big and red.

'You were generous to us once, *mon aviateur*,' he said. 'Ah, the generosity! – but it was for' – he looked round – 'murder!' he whispered dramatically.

'Are you suggesting that I hired you to kill the young woman who was found dead in Smith Street?' asked the other coolly. 'You were told not to kill.'

The man shrugged his shoulders again. 'She was drunk – we thought she was obstinate,' he said. 'How were we to know? Joseph gave her an extra squeeze, and, *voilà*! she was dead.'

Hermann eyed him as a naturalist might eye a new and a strange species of beetle. 'Suppose I say I will give you nothing?' he asked.

The big red hands were outstretched in pain. 'It would be unfortunate,' said the man, 'for you, for us, for all!' He seemed absurdly pleased with the rhyme of '*vous*', '*nous*', and '*tout*', and repeated it.

He was standing now an arm's length from the other. 'Are you very strong, my friend?' asked Hermann.

'I am considered so,' said the man complacently.

'*Attention!*' cried Hermann, and his small white hand shot out and gripped the visitor by the throat. He struggled, but he was in the hands of one who had had Le Cinq as a master, and Le Cinq was the greatest strangler of his day.

The fingers tightened on the other's throat, skilful fingers of steel that gripped the carotid artery and compressed the windpipe in one action. Down he went to the ground limply, then, when death stared at him, the fingers released their clutch. 'Get up,' said Hermann, and laughed noiselessly. The man staggered to his feet, fear in his eyes, his face blue and swollen. '*Mon Dieu!*' he gasped.

'Another minute, my infant,' said Hermann genially, 'and you would have been in hell. I do this to show you that I am better than you in your own profession. Years ago,' he went on reminiscently, 'your fellow countryman, Le Cinq, escaped from Devil's Island and came to New York. I paid him five thousand dollars to teach me to grip. You were in good hands, *ma foi!*'

The man stood shaking in every limb, his face twitching horribly, one hand feeling tenderly at his bruised throat.

'Here is a hundred pounds: if you wish, you may go to the police – but you must not come to me for money unless you have something to offer me for it. When I need you I will send for you. *Bonsoir.*'

'*Bonsoir, mon professeur!*' said the man with some remnants of his humour.

Hermann was flattered.

It was he who kept Martin Hubbard waiting, but Martin could afford to wait, though he had ordered dinner to be ready to the minute. Hermann found his host sitting patiently in the Palm Court of the Sweizerhof.

'Sorry to keep you, but I had an unexpected engagement – a pressing engagement,' he added with a smile.

'You millionaires!' said Martin Hubbard admiringly.

Handsome is a loose word applied to passable people, but Martin Hubbard had the features and the figure of a young Greek god. If his mouth was on the weak side, his small golden moustache was sufficient to hide it. Now, as he walked with his guest through the court, eyes were raised to watch him, eyes admiring, eyes approving, eyes resentful and suspicious.

Hermann Zeberlieff neither admired nor resented the good looks of his friend. Himself a man of striking appearance, with his youthful face and his superb strength visible in the breadth of shoulder and the set of his body, appearances were outside his philosophy. There were certain conventions which must be obeyed, certain ephemeral fashions which must be endured unless one wished to be regarded as eccentric, but he was satisfied to be advised as to these by competent authority.

His vanity ran in the direction of power: he was greedy for tribute to his wealth, his influence, and his position in the world of which he was a member.

'Here we are,' said Martin, and indicated a table.

Hermann glanced round the room and an ugly frown settled on his face. Three tables away sat King Kerry with a lady. From where he sat Hermann could not see her face, but a swift survey told him that since her gown was neither modish nor expensive, and her throat and hair were innocent of jewels, she was one of those pleasant nobodies whom King Kerry was always finding.

'Old Kerry and his secretary,' said Hubbard, following the direction of the other's eyes and desirous of finding an explanation for the frown.

Hermann looked at the girl with a new interest. His lips curled in a sarcastic smile as he remembered that, but for the luck of the game, this girl might have lain where the drunken daughter of her landlady was found.

He went through dinner talking on such events of the time as usually form the subject of prandial conversation. The real business of the meeting came later in the Palm Court when the two sat over their coffees and their cigarettes.

'Hubbard,' said the guest, 'I want you to marry my sister.'

He watched his man as he spoke, and saw a gleam of satisfaction come to the man's eyes.

'That's rather unexpected,' said Hubbard, stroking his moustache.

'I want you to marry her,' Hermann went on, taking no notice of the interruption, 'because I see no other way of getting her money.'

Hubbard looked across from under his brows and answered with no great show of geniality.

'Exactly what do you mean?'

'I shall explain what I mean,' said Hermann. 'But before we go any further I would ask that we have no exhibitions of high horse-riding, no family honour, or duties of gentlemen, or any of that highbrow nonsense, if you please.'

He said this quietly, but he was in sober earnest, and Hubbard checked a platitude which rose to his lips.

'Go on!' he said.

'I offer you a share of my sister's fortune – I offer you exceptional opportunities for meeting her, and I trust your singularly handsome person to do the rest.'

Hubbard caressed his moustache thoughtfully. 'Of course,' he said, 'if the lady is willing?'

'She isn't,' said Hermann frankly. 'She thinks that you are an insipid ass.' Mr Hubbard's face went very red. 'But she is young, and you haven't really had an opportunity of impressing your personality upon her.'

'Where do –' began Martin Hubbard a little stiffly.

'Listen,' commanded the other sharply, 'and for God's sake don't interrupt! By the terms of my father's will the sum of five million dollars is settled on the man she chooses to marry. Nobody knows this, except her and me and the lawyers. That sum represents about one half of the money which my father left to her. I want you to marry her and give me an agreement to pay me the sum of seven hundred and fifty thousand pounds on the day of your wedding.'

Calmly put, without anything in Hermann's tone to suggest that he was making a proposition out of the ordinary, it staggered his vis-a-vis. It did not stagger him sufficiently to make him forget that the arrangement was scarcely equitable.

'That is rather steep!' he demurred.

'That you should have a quarter of a million?' Hermann raised his eyebrows.

'I am not exactly a beggar, Zeberlieff,' said 'The Beauty', flushed and somewhat angry.

'You're not exactly a beggar,' agreed Hermann. 'You're a society sponge – now don't interrupt,' as Hubbard half rose from his seat. 'I am speaking plainly, but the occasion warrants it. Let us have no beating about the bush. You haven't a nickel to your name; you're on the Federated board because I put you there, and I put you there because I thought that sooner or later you would be useful. You are known from Mayfair to Pimlico as a fortune-hunter who has failed, and if you fail here you'll probably marry your landlady as an easy alternative to paying your arrears.'

Martin Hubbard's face went pink and white as the other continued with his insolent drawl. For the cursed thing about all that Hermann had said was that it was true – true even to the marked attention which the bourgeoise proprietress of his flat had paid to him. But if he was furious, as only a vain and hand-some man could be furious at such a humiliating experience, he had sense to see that a quarter of a million pounds was a fortune beyond his dreams.

'You're a damned Jew!' he growled, and Zeberlieff laughed.

'As a matter of fact, I have not a drop of Jewish blood in me,' he said. 'I often wish I had. I gather you accept?'

'Suppose she won't have anything to do with me?' asked the other.

'You must trust me,' said Hermann.

He stopped suddenly. King Kerry was coming toward him walking a little ahead of the girl he had been dining with. Even now Zeberlieff could not see her face, for from where he sat it was hidden by her escort's shoulder.

'Suppose –' Martin Hubbard was suggesting difficulties, but Hermann was not listening. He was curious to see the face of the girl whom Kerry had picked out from a crowd – according to report – to help him manipulate his millions.

They were nearly abreast of the two men when Kerry slackened his pace and for the first time Hermann Zeberlieff looked upon the face of Elsie Marion.

He leapt up from his chair as if he had been shot. His face was white and drawn, and beads of perspiration stood on his temples as he pointed a trembling finger at the startled girl.

'You – you!' he croaked hoarsely, and fell fainting to the ground.

CHAPTER XVII

To the General Public –

I have recently acquired the business known as Tack and Brighten, and this is to give notice that I intend carrying on that business on new lines and by new methods under the title of Kerry's Stores. I have quadrupled the variety of stock, which now includes every kind of ladies' and children's outfitting and men's hosiery.

There is no article of ready-made attire, no material which may be purchased in Oxford Street, which is not to be found in the Kerry Store.

The building has undergone extensive alterations, a new tea lounge has been added, two powerful electric elevators have been erected, and a rest room has been built on the first floor.

To inaugurate this business I announce a half-price sale year. For twelve months from today you will be able to purchase goods for exactly half of what you pay for the same goods in any other shop in Oxford Street.

Nor is this all.

Three shifts of employers will attend to customers, and the shop will be open day and night – except on Sundays and for two hours daily. All goods will be marked in the figures at which they are sold in other establishments and the following reductions will be made.

Purchasers between 10 a.m. and 8 p.m., the article may be had at half the marked price. From 8 p.m. to 11 p.m. at 55 per cent reduction; from 11 p.m. to 1 a.m. 60 per cent; and from 1 a.m. to 8 a.m. 65 per cent reduction. From 8 till 10 the Store will be in the hands of the cleaners.

Example: Article marked 10s.

From 10 a.m. to 8 p.m. our price is 5s.

From 8 p.m. to 11 p.m. our price 4s. 6d.

From 11 p.m. to 1 p.m. our price 4s.

From 1 a.m. to 8 a.m. our price 3s. 6d.

You will be waited upon by a staff which is paid higher wages and works shorter hours than any other staff in London. Everything will be marked in plain figures. Choose your goods in the sample room – they will be delivered in the rest room.

This advertisement will appear for three days, at the end of which time the Store will be advertising itself.

Yours faithfully,

KING KERRY.

P.S. – I am actually giving away a minimum £300,000 in the course of the next twelve months; it is open for you to take your share. There is no chance of our stock running short. I have ten of the greatest firms of manufacturers under contract to deliver me goods to the value of £600,000 for the half-year ending December twenty-three, and to the value of £800,000 for the following half-year.

The advertisement occupied a full page of the most important of the available full pages in every newspaper in London. It was on a Monday that the first intimation of the sale appeared in the shape of a great poster on every hoarding of the metropolis. The announcement was simple to a point of baldness.

KERRY'S STORE, 989–997, OXFORD STREET, W.
MADAM, – Any article of wear you may see in the window of any drapery store or ladies' outfitters in Oxford Street may

be purchased from my store on and after Monday next at exactly half the price, and even less. See Wednesday's newspapers for particulars.

                              KING KERRY.

This, in huge letters, confronted the citizens of London wherever they walked abroad. It faced them in the tube trains and in the tube lifts. It was plastered on railway stations and covered the ends of dead walls. It was printed in a modified form on the back of tram tickets and on the boards of buses and cars. Sandwich men in hundreds perambulated London bearing this announcement. It appeared unexpectedly on the screens of cinemas, was to be found in theatre programmes and even crept into the pages of parish magazines.

A week later came the newspaper advertising, and at eleven o'clock on the morning there was formed the most extraordinary queue that London had ever seen. It began forming at seven o'clock in the morning. At nine o'clock reserves of 'E' division were called out to marshal the line. Four deep the queue stretched from Kerry's Store to New Oxford Street, a distance of a mile and a quarter.

There was no doubt in the mind of the thrifty Londoner that the goods were of the quality stated. Endless velvet belts had for three days displayed samples of the treasures within. Still less was there any question as to the willingness of the munificent proprietor to allow all these goods to go out at half price. There was some doubt in the public mind as to how long these sacrifices would go on.

The doors opened at eleven, and Kerry's system worked with the utmost smoothness. As fast as customers were supplied they went out through the new doors at the rear of the building. They learnt that they must come on any future occasion with their minds made up as to the article they desired. Once they had passed from the sample room to the rest chamber above they were not re-admitted. If they remembered something they had wanted they must take their place in the queue again.

Every class of society was represented in that mammoth bargain hunt. Motor cars dropped their befurred occupants to walk side by side with the dingy little woman from the poorer streets of the East and South. Women with command of capital went in with well-filled purses and came out proudly conscious of the fact that they had bought double supplies for the price of one.

At three o'clock in the afternoon the queue was a quarter of a mile long, at ten o'clock at night some fifteen hundred people were moving slowly to the doors, and when two o'clock struck a queue of respectable dimensions still waited for the extra reductions.

'It is wonderful!'

Elsie surveyed the sight from an upper window of the store at half-past one in the morning. The street behind the building was filled with motor lorries and vans which had brought up fresh supplies from the warehouse which King Kerry had taken in South London, and whilst one gang of men was busily unloading, another was stripping the packing cases and sorting out the contents for delivery in the wrapping room on the fourth floor.

King Kerry, smoking a cigar, was by her side.

'We're doing fine,' he said. 'We can't have lost more than a thousand pounds. We may not have lost that.

'My idea is that we shall drop something like a thousand a day,' he went on, 'but the margin of profit on these kinds of goods is so large that we might easily lose nothing after the system has shaken down.'

There were other spectators equally interested. Leete and Zeberlieff sat in the shadowy interior of the latter's car and watched the midnight queue. 'How long will this farce last?' growled Leete.

The other made no reply. He looked ill and weary. There were little lines about his eyes which were unusual in him. He looked malignantly at the building which shielded his enemy. So that was why he had chosen his secretary from the crowd. Because she had resembled to a miraculous degree the girl whose death lay at Hermann's door.

There had been tragedy there – for the girl. Hermann had been embarrassed, but no more. It had widened the breach with King Kerry, for the grey man – who was not grey in those days – had loved the child in his way. Even Hermann credited that way with being all that was benevolent and sweet. She was a child in King's eyes, scarcely emerged from the doll and candy stage when all Boston had awakened with a shock to the knowledge that she was indeed a woman, with a woman's capacity for joy, a woman's fore-ordained measure of sorrow.

'He can't keep this up,' Leete was saying, and Hermann turned with a start from his bitter memories.

'Can't!' he said savagely. 'He can and will – you don't know him. He's a damned Yankee magnate – you've never dealt with that kind before, I guess! Can't! Don't you bank on his giving up. Has it affected Goulding's?'

'Affected it!' the other laughed harshly. 'I doubt if we've taken ten pounds today, and the running expenses of the place are from forty to fifty a day. I'll apply for an injunction to stop this queue – it's illegal.'

'And advertise him?' asked Hermann; 'give him a gratuitous ad? Nothing doing! We've got to find another way.'

He bit his nails in thought, his eyes watching the slow-moving procession of customers as it moved before the gaily lit store.

'Suppose this goes on,' he asked, 'and your takings dwindle to ten pounds or less, what will be the result?'

Mr Leete swallowed something in the darkness.

'Ruin,' he said; 'we should go under. We couldn't afford to compete, we should pay no dividends, for we've no reserves. And it won't only be us – there are half a dozen firms in the neighbourhood who are worse off than we. They would all go smash.'

'Suppose you all agree to sell your stuff in competition?'

Leete shook his head with an oath.

'What is the use of talking? There is a fact we can't get over. He can afford to throw a million pounds into the gutter – we can't. Who is going to finance a business under the present conditions? There isn't a City house which would lend us a red cent till it is definitely known what is the limit of King Kerry's operations. Our only hope is that he gets tired.'

'He'll not get tired,' said the other.

He glanced round along the pavement by the side of which the car was drawn up. A little group of sightseers were watching the strange scene of London's midnight shopping. One of these was a young man whose face Hermann remembered having seen before. For a little time he couldn't 'place' the stranger, then he remembered that he had seen him in Park Lane.

This was Vera's gallant young student. He was alone apparently and was watching with every evidence of interest the remarkable happening. Near by stood another young man, smoking a cigar and watching the proceedings with an approving eye.

CHAPTER XVIII

To think was to act with Hermann Zeberlieff. He must chance whether Vera had antagonized the youth. He stepped out of the car and made his way to where Gordon Bray stood. 'I think we have met before,' he greeted him, and the cordiality which his appearance excited dispelled any doubt as to the other's attitude of mind.

They stood chatting for a little while, discussing the peculiarities of King Kerry. 'Don't you think he is very wonderful?' asked the enthusiast.

'Very,' replied Hermann dryly.

'He is such a splendid fellow to his employees, too,' the young man went on, utterly oblivious of the fact that no word in praise of King Kerry was calculated to arouse a responsive glow in the breast of the other. 'I met Elsie Marion at lunch today.'

'Elsie Marion?' repeated Hermann with obvious interest.

Gordon nodded.

'Yes, she is his secretary, you know; we used to live under the same roof' – he smiled – 'before Elsie made good.'

'And what has she to say about this great man?' asked Hermann, with gentle irony.

The young man laughed. 'I'm afraid I'm a little too enthused,' he said, 'and probably you being an American and used to the hustle and enterprise of your fellow-countrymen, are not so struck as I am with his methods.'

'I am immensely struck by them,' replied Hermann, but did not mean exactly what the other meant. 'I should like to have a talk with you, Mr Bray; there are so many matters we could discuss. They tell me you were in court when my sister was sentenced.'

The young man turned and surveyed him with grave eyes. 'Yes,' he said quietly.

'It was an awful pity, don't you think, that she should make such a fool of herself?' asked Hermann. Gordon Bray flushed.

'I think she must have had a very excellent reason for doing it,' he said.

The other concealed a smile. Here was a devoted swain indeed, one of the 'worship at a distance' brigade he placed him, a tame dog to be petted or kicked by the wealthy woman who had the patience to keep him to heel.

'It is a matter of opinion,' he said aloud; 'personally, I detest the Suffragette, and it was a revelation and a shock to discover that my sister could be included in their numbers; but that is beside the point. Will you come along and have a chat?'

'When?' asked the other.

'There is no time like the present,' said Mr Zeberlieff good-humouredly.

The young man stared.

'But it is rather late, isn't it?' he said.

'Not at all,' said the other, 'if you can spare the time.'

He walked back and introduced the youth to his companion, and Mr Leete submitted with bad grace to the presence of a third party at a moment when he intended sounding Zeberlieff as to his willingness to help finance Goulding's against the competition which had come to them.

They dropped Leete at his flat and went on to Park Lane, and in Hermann's little study the two men settled down to cigarettes and coffee, which was served with such little delay as to suggest that the excellent Martin had produced the liquid part of the entertainment from a thermos flask.

'I'm coming straight to the point with you, Mr Bray,' said Hermann after a while. 'I'm a very rich man, as you possibly know, and you, as far as I am able to judge, have not too much of this world's wealth.'

Gordon Bray nodded. 'That is perfectly true,' he said quietly.

'Now I am willing to serve you if you will serve me,' Hermann went on. 'You possibly know that my sister is engaged.'

There was a little pause, and then Gordon said in so low a voice that the other hardly heard him – 'No, I did not know this.'

Hermann looked at him sharply.

'Yes, she is engaged all right, to my friend Martin Hubbard – you may have heard of him; he is one of the best known men in town, and is especially precious to me, since he has the same name as my servant, and I never forget him,' he smiled.

Up till then Hermann had not dreamt that he was, in any way, hurting the feelings of the other. It never occurred to him that this man of the people should harbour any serious thought of love for the woman who was so far beyond his reach. Something in the young man's face arrested him, and he glanced suspiciously at his visitor. 'I hope my sister's engagement has your approval,' he said with good-natured irony.

'It is not for me to approve or disapprove,' said the young man calmly. 'I can only express the hope that she will be very happy.'

Whatever suspicion might have been in Hermann's mind was dissipated by the attitude of the other.

'I don't suppose that she will be very happy,' he said carelessly. 'After all, happiness is a relative term. A woman with a couple of million pounds in her own right can find happiness where a less fortunate creature –'

'How can I help you?' interrupted Gordon. He had to say something. It seemed to him that the beating of his heart could be heard in the room, and the horrible sense of depression which had come to him when the other broke the news was patent in his face.

'I have reason to know,' said Hermann slowly, 'that my sister has a very high opinion of your judgement. I seem to remember that she has spoken to me several times about you. It very often happens,' he went on with an insolent disregard for the other's feelings, 'that girls of my sister's class are considerably influenced by the advice of men of your class, and I believe this is so in the case of my sister and yourself. You can help me a great deal,' he said emphatically, 'if, when my sister comes out, when she recovers her normal position in society, you use whatever influence you possess to further this marriage. I expect,' he went on thoughtfully, 'she will kick up a row when she finds that I have arranged her affairs for her.'

'Then she doesn't know?' interrupted the other quickly.

'Not yet,' replied Hermann. 'You see, my sister is a very extraordinary girl; she has been a source of great trouble to me during the years I have been responsible for her well-being. You will understand, Mr Bray, as a man of the world, something of my responsibility, and my anxiety to see her happily settled in life. At present, with her independence, and with her enormous fortune,' he spoke emphatically, tapping the polished surface of the table before him with every sentence, 'she is the prey of every fortune-hunter who happens along. My friend Hubbard is a man against whom such a charge could not lie.'

He was depending upon Gordon Bray being perfectly innocent of the gossip in which society indulged; that he knew nothing of the shaking heads which followed Martin Hubbard's advent to the drawing rooms of Mayfair, or the elaborate care with which the mothers and the aunts of eligible wards withdrew their charges at the first opportunity.

Gordon Bray made no response. If he knew any of these things he did not betray the fact. He sat in the soft cushioned chair, facing the other, and was silent. Hermann Zeberlieff made the mistake of confusing his silence with acquiescence, and continued –

'I am willing to give you whatever chance you want in the world,' he said slowly, 'in return for your good offices. On the day my sister marries I am prepared to give you a couple of thousand pounds – a very considerable sum, and one which would assist you materially to reach that place in the world which I have no doubt as an ambitious young man you have set yourself to attain.'

Again Bray did not answer. He was looking at the other, relief in his heart, contempt for the man before him occupying his thoughts. To have asked him of all people in the world to assist in coercing this dream lady of his! He could have laughed at the grotesque absurdity of it. As it was, he waited until Hermann had concluded his expression of views upon the responsibility of safeguarding the millionairess before he spoke. Then he rose, and reached out for his hat, which he had placed upon a chair near by.

'There's no necessity for your going,' said Hermann in surprise.

'Nevertheless, I am going,' answered the other. 'I'm afraid, Mr Zeberlieff, you have made a great mistake in confiding so much to me, but you may be sure that I shall respect your confidence.'

Hermann lowered his brows.

'What do you mean?' he asked harshly.

'Just what I say,' said Gordon Bray quietly. 'You ask me to do the kind of work which it would be disgraceful and discreditable to do even if I had no' – he hesitated – 'no friendship for your sister.'

'You refuse – why?' asked Hermann in surprise.

It was indeed a matter for surprise that this man, who at best was only a superior type of clerk, should throw away an opportunity of earning two thousand pounds.

'If I were strong enough to influence Miss Zeberlieff,' the young man went on, 'it would not be in the direction of Mr Martin Hubbard, or any other human being in the world, that I would influence her.'

'Why?' asked Hermann again.

'Because I love her,' said his visitor calmly, 'and because I believe she loves me.'

If somebody had thrown a bomb into the room Hermann Zeberlieff could not have been more surprised than he was.

'You love her,' he repeated incredulously; 'how absurd!' Something in the young man's face should have warned him, but he went on – 'No, no, my good man,' he said with an unpleasant smile. 'You must find another easy way to wealth than marrying my sister. So that was the idea of –'

'Stop!' Gordon Bray took a step towards him, his eyes bright with anger. 'I don't allow you or any other man to say that sort of thing,' he said. 'I can make allowances for your anger. I can well imagine that I am not the sort of man that you would care to have as a brother-in-law. At the same time, it is only fair to say,' he went on, 'that you are the very last type of man in the world that I should have chosen for the same office. I love your sister, and I am going to marry her, but I am not going to marry her until I have secured some sort of position in the world for myself, without her aid, save for such help and inspiration as her splendid character will give me.'

'Excuse me if I laugh,' interrupted Hermann. He had got back to himself with extraordinary quickness.

'Without her aid,' the young man went on, ignoring the insult, 'I am going to establish a place for myself in the world, and when I have I shall take her. As to the proposal you make, in which Mr Hubbard plays so prominent a part, I most strongly advise you to put that matter entirely out of your head.' He was bold now, bold with the sense of power.

Hermann's face was not good to look upon. He was desperate – desperate in the knowledge of his own perilous position if his plans for securing something of his sister's fortune were frustrated.

Zeberlieff's command over himself was marvellous. Shocked as he was, beaten as he might well be, he pulled himself together with an effort and smiled. 'If my sister has to wait until you establish a position in London,' he said, 'I am afraid you will be marrying a middle-aged woman.'

'That may be,' said the other quietly; 'but if Mr King Kerry –'

'King Kerry,' repeated Hermann quickly; 'is he in this scheme too?'

'Mr King Kerry knows nothing about the matter,' said the young man, 'but he has promised me an opportunity just as soon as he starts building.' He stopped.

'He starts building – what?' asked Hermann quickly. 'What is he going to build; what is the great idea; where is he going to pull down and build? Tell me that!'

'I can tell you nothing,' said the other, and walked to the door.

'I ask you one question.' Hermann stood by the fireplace, his elbow resting upon the marble mantelpiece, his head on his hand. 'Will you swear to me that my sister loves you?'

It was an unexpected question, and almost took Gordon's breath away by reason of its unlikeliness.

'I cannot swear to that,' he smiled; 'yet I believe it.'

'She has told you?' Gordon nodded. 'Then that is all right,' smiled Hermann. 'Now I will show you out.'

He led the way downstairs. On the ground floor was the dining room and his little library.

'Perhaps you would like to drink the health of my sister?' he said.

Gordon hesitated. He had evidently done this man an injustice.

'I should indeed,' he said genially, and Hermann led the way into the dining room, closing the door behind him.

He walked to a little cupboard and took out a quart black bottle and two tiny glasses. 'This is the most powerful liqueur in the world – Van der Merwe. We will drink to my sister's release – and our better acquaintance.'

'With all the pleasure in life,' said the young man heartily.

First Hermann poured a glass full of the amber-coloured fluid and handed it to his guest, then he filled his own glass, and Gordon could know nothing of the tiny black button halfway down the neck that the other had pressed when the first glass had been poured.

The presence of that button had been sufficient to discharge into the glass a minute quantity of a colourless liquid.

'Good luck!' said Hermann, and drank his glassful.

Gordon followed suit.

'And now,' said Hermann easily, 'you must sit down and smoke a cigarette whilst I tell you something of Vera.'

His narrative had not proceeded far before Gordon Bray's head sank on his breast, and he fell back in the chair, in which the other had placed him, in a dreamless sleep.

CHAPTER XIX

On the opposite side of the road a young man, smoking the end of a cigar, his felt hat on the back of his head, and his hands thrust deep into his heavy overcoat pockets, waited patiently for Gordon Bray to come out. The light had gone out in the upstairs sitting room nearly an hour ago. Whither had they adjourned?

He lit another cigar, and prepared for an extension of his vigil. A reporter with his heart in his work counts neither time nor hardship as wasted if he can secure a story. And this young reporter of the *Evening Herald* was no exception to the general rule.

He waited, chatting with such policemen as passed. Half-past four came, and with it the pearl-grey of dawning daylight, but still nobody came out from the ornamental door of 410, Park Lane. Five, six, and seven came, and the world began to wake up drowsily, and the early morning populace of London went hurrying north and south along the fashionable thoroughfare.

'He can't be staying the night,' muttered the young reporter.

He scribbled a note and sent it off by the first likely messenger, and in half an hour a man came briskly down Park Lane until he reached the place where the watcher stood.

'You can go off now,' he said.

'I don't want to go off until I've seen this thing through,' said the reporter.

'Do you think he went in?' asked the newcomer.

'I'm sure,' said the other emphatically. 'I followed them in a taxi-cab. They dropped old Leete in Piccadilly and came on here. I saw him get out. I saw the car drive off, and, moreover, the two men go in. I've been watching ever since.'

'Is there a back way?' asked the other.

'No – the servants' entrance is in the basement, down the flight of stairs here to the left.'

He indicated the area.

At seven-thirty from this same area there issued a man who was evidently a servant. The reporter crossed the road and followed him up Park Lane, quickening his pace until he came abreast of them. 'Excuse me,' he said.

The man-servant, Martin, turned with surprise.

'Do you want me?' he asked civilly; then, with a change of expression to one of pleasant recognition he said: 'You're the reporter who came to the house about Miss Zeberlieff, aren't you?'

The young man nodded. 'Guilty,' he said with a smile. 'Any news of her?'

'She's coming out today,' said the man. 'I can't understand it; as nice a lady as ever drew breath.' He shook his head mournfully.

'I suppose you'll be glad to see her back, won't you?'

'She won't come back to the house,' said Martin emphatically. 'Her maid has taken all her things to a hotel. I don't suppose she likes the idea of returning after what has happened,' he speculated. 'That's all I can tell you,' he said, and was moving off with a nod.

'One minute,' said the reporter; 'you're in a hurry to get away when a poor devil of a reporter wants to earn a few shillings from you.'

The man grinned. 'I wish I earned as many shillings as you earned pounds,' he said enviously. 'I shouldn't be working for him.' He jerked his head in the direction of the house.

'I suppose it isn't exactly lively?' suggested the reporter.

The man shook his head.

'We haven't had a guest for goodness knows how long,' he said. 'He brought a chap home last night, but he was gone again in an hour. There were times when –' He checked himself, thinking perhaps he was saying too much, else he might have given a very graphic resume of a period in Mr Zeberlieff's social life when guests were frequent and sovereign tips were of daily occurrence.

'Did he stay the night?' asked the reporter carelessly.

'Who?' demanded the man.

'The gentleman who came to the house last night.'

The servant shook his head.

'I tell you, he was only there an hour, and I never as much as opened the door to him.'

'Is Mr Zeberlieff up yet?' asked the reporter.

'It's no good going to him,' said the servant hastily, 'and if you do, for the Lord's sake, don't mention that I've been chatting with you. Yes, he's up; as a matter of fact, he hasn't been in bed. He sent me to bed at two, and he's been up writing most of the night. Anyhow, he hasn't worried me.'

He held a letter in his hand, and was evidently taking it to the post.

'He writes a curious hand,' said the reporter, half to himself.

The man lifted the letter up and eyed it critically.

'I don't know – it isn't so bad,' he said. 'I've known worse.'

In that second the journalist had read the name and the address, and had all his work cut out to suppress the whistle which was part of the ritual of surprise.

'Well,' he said, with seeming reluctance, 'if he's been up all night he won't want to see me; anyway, I'll go up to Holloway and meet Miss Zeberlieff,' and with a nod the men parted.

The reporter strolled leisurely across the road and joined his relief. 'You can hang on here,' he said, 'but I don't think you'll see anything. I'm going home to have a bath and then get into communication with King Kerry.'

'What is up?' asked the other man.

'I don't know yet,' was the reply. 'You just watch the house and let me know – and if Bray comes out, follow him. But I especially want to know if Zeberlieff himself goes out.'

Inside the house in Park Lane, Hermann Zeberlieff was walking thoughtfully up and down his drawing room. He had bathed and showed no evidence of his absence from bed save for the tiny lines about his eyes, which really owed their existence to quite another cause. He looked fresh and bright and eminently handsome in the searching light of the morning sun. Martin came to summon him to breakfast, and was pouring out the coffee for him when Hermann said suddenly –

'Oh, by the way, Martin, you wanted to go down into Cornwall to see your people the other day.'

'Yes, sir,' said the servant; 'but you couldn't spare me, sir.'

'I can spare you now,' said Hermann. 'You can go by the eleven train this morning.'

The man looked at him in astonishment. 'And have you made arrangements, sir, as to who will look after you while I'm away?'

'I shall go to a hotel,' said Hermann carelessly. 'You're not exactly indispensable, Martin.'

'Of course not, sir,' said the dutiful servant. 'I beg your pardon, sir.' The man hesitated.

'Well?'

'I've lost the key of the wine cellar somewhere,' said Martin apologetically. 'I laid it down on the hall table last night and forgot all about it.'

'Don't bother, I've a key of my own,' said Zeberlieff.

'I can get it open easily,' said the man.

'I don't want you to go anywhere near the wine cellar,' said Zeberlieff sharply. 'Who was that man I saw you speaking with?'

The guilty Martin went red.

'He's a reporter, sir,' he stammered. 'He came to enquire about Miss Zeberlieff.'

'H'm!' said Hermann. 'I don't want you to chat with that kind of people. I told you before.'

'Well, sir –' began the man.

'I understand about Miss Zeberlieff. What did you tell him?'

'I told him, sir, that we could give him no information whatso-ever,' said the unveracious Martin glibly, 'and I forbade him ever to speak to me in the street again.'

'Admirable liar!' responded Hermann with a little smile. 'He asked nothing else?'

'Nothing, sir,' answered the man emphatically.

'I don't like reporters,' Hermann went on, 'they have not exactly been mascots to me. About the wine cellar,' he said, after a pause, 'I suppose you want to take a sample of my port to your Cornish friends?'

The man was too used to the insults of the other to be over-much hurt; but he was very angry indeed.

Hermann was unusually cheerful during the morning, though his servant strode about with a black face and did only what work was required of him. He did not go near the wine cellar, nor did he think it worth his while to report to his master that in some mysterious way a big oaken arm-chair had disappeared from the study.

'He'll probably think I've taken that to Cornwall, too!' muttered the man.

At a quarter to eleven a taxi-cab was called to 410, Park Lane, and Martin's luggage was deposited on top. An interested reporter of the *Evening Herald* – he had been at one time a bright and particular star on *The Monitor* – watched the departure with mixed feelings, and when a quarter of an hour later Hermann himself issued from the house and closed the door carefully behind him, he was followed at a respectful distance by two men, neither of whom was the reporter.

CHAPTER XX

Vera Zeberlieff had been released from prison that morning with a batch of other Suffragettes, and had laughingly declined the official welcome which the political enthusiasts had prepared at a restaurant in Holborn.

She had looked around eagerly when she emerged from the prison gates for one face, but it was not there. She felt a sense of disappointment out of all proportion, as she told herself, to the need of the occasion. She remembered that he had his living to earn, that he might find it very embarrassing to obtain the necessary leave to meet a friend coming from prison. She smiled to herself at the thought. He would hardly lie. He was not that kind of man, and herein her estimate of Gordon Bray was an accurate one.

The taxi she hailed carried her to the hotel where she had engaged a suite, and there she found a tearful maid awaiting her. A few brusque but kindly words dried the tears and stemmed the flow, and arrested, too, a volume of altogether mistaken sympathy which the girl had prepared.

'I will have some breakfast,' said Vera.

She felt happy and strong, and her healthy young spirit had enabled her to overcome the little twinge of depression which had been hers at the disappointment of not seeing the man who loved her.

There were innumerable letters waiting for her; she singled out one directed in her brother's writing; it was very brief. There was no word of recrimination, no reproach. The tone was one almost of cordiality. He told her that he would call upon her at half-past eleven on the morning of her release, and he asked her to be so kind as to afford him this opportunity for an interview. It was a most correct epistle.

She could do no less, she thought; and gave instructions that he was to be announced the moment he arrived.

King Kerry sent a cheerful little note of welcome, and this and the conventional expressions of approval or disapproval which her conduct had called for from her numerous friends constituted her correspondence. At half-past eleven Hermann came, and was shown up into the sitting room. He did not offer his hand, nor did he take the chair which she offered him.

'Well, Vera,' he said, 'I think we might as well understand each other now. I am going to make some very startling confessions, which, since you and I are alone, and we have got to start afresh, it is both expedient and necessary for me to make. In the first place, you will not be surprised to learn,' he smiled, 'that if you had died before the second portion of the legacy became due I should not have been particularly sorry.'

She nodded, and surveyed him strangely.

'Does it occur to you,' she asked, 'that if you, on the other hand, had died before the legacy became due, that I should not have mourned to any great extent; and do you also realize that I should have benefited considerably by such a death?'

He looked at her startled. Was she of that kind? It could not be possible, he thought; but she was jesting, he saw the laughter in her eyes, her mocking merriment at his surprise.

'Since we are both homicidal,' he said humorously, 'there is very little to be made in the way of confession. Now that you have inherited your money, and I understand you saw your solicitor in gaol –'

She agreed with an inclination of her head.

'Nothing is gained by me, unless, of course,' again with that sly smile, 'you've executed a will in my favour.'

'You must never regard that project with any certainty,' she remarked.

'So I gathered,' he said. 'Therefore, as far as I can see, the only chance I have of securing any of this money which you have, and which is so necessary to me – I beg you to believe that – is to find a husband for you.'

She laughed, but watched him narrowly. 'My dear Hermann,' she said, 'you've been engaged in that excellent pastime for quite a while.'

'And at last I have succeeded,' he said.

'You have succeeded, have you?'

The irony in her voice appealed to him.

'I have succeeded,' he said complacently, and sat down. 'You are going to marry my young friend, Martin Hubbard.'

She made a little gesture of disgust.

'You will have the satisfaction of knowing that he is the handsomest man in London, that he descends from William the Conqueror, and that he has the entrée into all the best society. He is perfectly educated – Eton and Balliol, though as to that I am not sure – and, last but not least, he plays a very excellent game of double dummy.'

'Are there any other virtues which you have overlooked?' she asked.

'None,' said Hermann – 'that are known to me,' he added.

'Of course,' she said, 'there is something behind all this, and you know as well as I that I would no more think of marrying your freakish friend than I should think of marrying your butler.'

'Or one of your pupils,' suggested Hermann pleasantly.

She frowned.

'My pupils! I don't quite understand.'

'I mean one of those excellent students of yours at the technical college to whom, in your large benevolence, you award, from time to time, gold medals and finely engraved diplomas of merit. That also would be a preposterous marriage, would it not?'

She flushed slightly.

'So you know, do you?' she asked coolly. 'Preposterous or not, I think it is a more likely marriage.'

'With the admirable Mr – I forget his name.'

'With the admirable Mister whose name you forget,' she rejoined.

'That makes it rather awkward for me,' he said thoughtfully, 'and it makes it rather awkward for the admirable Mister –. You see, I've a working arrangement with Martin Hubbard. He gives me a cheque for seven hundred and fifty thousand pounds the day you are married. Do you get me?'

'I get you,' she said. 'I guessed there was some such an arrangement. You are the last person in the world I should imagine who would play the part of a disinterested matchmaker.'

'Right you are!' he said heartily. 'You can avoid a great many unpleasant consequences – and, incidentally, one of these is Martin Hubbard – if in a fit of generosity you gave me your cheque for the same amount, or would instruct your lawyer to cause the transfer of stock to this value from your account to mine.'

She laughed, though she was not amused.

'I think we have gone a little too far,' she said. 'Now, will you speak openly what you mean and exactly what you want?'

'You know what I want,' he said in his most businesslike tone. 'I want you to marry Martin Hubbard because I greatly desire three-quarters of a million pounds, being seventy-five per cent of the portion which comes to your husband under our father's will. Failing that, I want the money. I don't care whether you have a husband or not. I have sense enough to realize that Martin would be rather a trial – and, anyway, he is not worth two hundred and fifty thousand pounds.'

'I see,' she said; then: 'You may be as assured that I shall not be Mrs Hubbard as you can be that you will not have one single dollar of the money.'

'Are you so sure?' he asked.

'I am pretty sure,' she said coolly.

There was a little pause.

'Are you fond of this Mr – ?

'Mr Gordon Bray,' she supplied the name.

'Are you very fond of him?' he repeated.

She eyed him steadily.

'I fail to see that that is any business of yours,' she replied, 'but since there is no reason in the world why I should not tell you, I must admit that I am very fond of him and that he is very fond of me.'

'How perfectly ideal,' said Hermann with mock ecstasy. 'I can see King Kerry making two columns of it in his new paper – "The Romance of a Technical School: Millionairess weds Technical Student. The honeymoon to be spent at Margate, in deference to the bridegroom's wishes."'

She was silent under his gibes, for she knew that the real issue had to come. He would show his hand presently; it was like Hermann to wax jovial when the business ahead was sinister. She had a little worried feeling that her troubles were not over.

'If you are really fond of this young man,' he said deliberately, 'at what figure do you value his life?'

'So that is it?'

Her face was pale: the peril which had confronted her all these years had never been so terrible to contemplate or caused so tight a clutch upon her heart as the knowledge that her brother would strike at her through the man she loved.

'Come, put a value on him. None of your King Kerry half-price values,' he said, with his musical laugh, 'but the full market value of a human life that is very precious to you. Shall we say three-quarters of a million?'

There surged up in her heart such a rising flood of hate against this smiling man who had tortured her for so many years, who had striven to take her life for the wealth which might accrue to him. It was a hate which blotted out and blinded all other considerations than this present fact: here before her stood the man who had caused untold misery to hundreds of his fellows, the man who had cornered food necessities, who had wrecked lives, who had ridden roughshod over susceptibilities, who had gained his pleasure at the cost of breaking hearts.

The touch of devil which was within him was within her also. They came from a common stock, and perhaps it was old Grandfather Zeberlieff, that remorseless man, who spoke in her heart now.

She had an inspiration, the hate that raged within her sharpened her perception and made her see very clearly that which she had not seen before. Upon the inspiration she acted: she went to her desk and opened the drawer.

He watched her with some amusement. It is curious how in such moments the brain works upon such magnificent materials.

She found herself calculating what would be the cost of the damage done to the wall – whether they would turn her out of the hotel; but whatever might be the consequences, big or little, she was prepared to face it.

She knew Hermann at that moment as she had never known him before.

'At what do you value the price of your lover's life?' he asked again.

'I couldn't tell you,' she said.

She took something from the drawer and handled it.

It was a revolver.

He frowned.

'We are getting melodramatic,' he said, and the words were hardly out of his mouth when the pistol exploded and a shot whizzed past his head.

He staggered back, pale to the lips.

'My God, what are you doing?' he gasped in that shrill high voice of his which invariably betrayed his distress.

She smiled as sweetly as ever Zeberlieff had smiled in a moment of such crisis.

'I am so sorry,' she said. 'I trust I haven't hurt you.'

He stared at her in mortal terror for the space of a minute, and then walked quickly to the door.

'Stop!' she said.

There was something in her voice which claimed his obedience.

'What do you want?' he asked shakily.

'I want to tell you,' she said quietly, 'that if any harm comes to Gordon Bray I will kill you, that is all. Now, get out!'

He needed no second telling, and was halfway down the stairs when he met the excited manager of the hotel running up to discover the cause for a pistol shot – an occurrence which even the occupation of a private sitting room did not justify.

It was easy to explain; much easier for a lady known to be enormously rich, and the relieved manager bowed himself out.

She took from the drawer where the revolver again reposed a little case and opened it. On the one side was a portrait of their father, and on the other a photographic study of Gordon Bray taken by one of the technical students.

She looked at the clear-cut face and shook her head.

'Poor dear,' she said whimsically, half to herself, 'you are marrying into a queer family!'

CHAPTER XXI

Zeberlieff hurried back to Park Lane, shaken and panic-stricken. Never before in his life had anything affected him as it had at the moment when he had seen the pistol barrel turned slowly in his direction, and had known before the shot was fired that it was being aimed at him. He remembered now that she was a most excellent revolver shot.

Was it by accident she missed him?

He might have spared himself the trouble of speculating. If she had intended killing him, he would have been dead. He was afraid of her now – more afraid because she was the one human in the world of whom he was in terror at any time. She was now a terrifying figure.

He had one intention, and that to release Gordon Bray from the wine cellar, where he was at that moment secured hand and foot to a heavy oaken chair.

He found Leete waiting on the doorstep, and inwardly cursed him; but he could not afford to be impolite. He wanted every friend he could muster now.

'I've been waiting for an hour,' grumbled Leete. 'Where the devil are all your servants?'

'They're all out,' said the other. 'Come in.'

He unlocked the door, and ushered Leete into the dining room, on the ground floor.

'What is the news?'

'Oh, he's at it again,' said Leete despairingly. 'He isn't satisfied with ruining our business in Oxford Street, but he's bought up a huge block of buildings along one side of Regent Street, and he has bought the Hilarity Theatre. Why, soon, the man will own the best part of London.'

'You haven't come all the way to tell me that, have you?' asked Hermann.

'No, there's something else. That young man you introduced me to last night –'

'What about him?' asked Hermann quickly.

'Well, the police have been round to see me.'

'The police!' Zeberlieff changed colour.

'Yes. It appears that he hasn't been home all night. He was seen to go into your house, and since then all trace has been lost of him.'

'Who saw him go in?' asked Zeberlieff.

'A reporter on Kerry's paper. They brought me round a proof of the story they're going to run in this evening's edition. Would you like to see it?'

'Tell me what it is – quickly!' said Hermann.

'Oh, it's a sensational story,' said the other disparagingly. 'They describe it as the remarkable disappearance of a young man who accompanied the famous Mr Zeberlieff to his house and did not come out again. It appears the reporter followed you and has been watching the house all night.'

Zeberlieff bit his lip.

'So that was what he was talking to my servant about, was it?' he said; and then, seeing that the other man was regarding him curiously, he turned with a laugh.

'My dear chap, what should I know about this man? All that I can tell you is that he came here and he was rather impertinent. I don't mind confessing to you that he went as far as to say that he wanted to marry my sister – an altogether preposterous suggestion. So I kicked him out,' he continued airily.

Leete sniffed.

'The unfortunate thing is,' he said, 'that nobody saw you kick him out. That's where all the trouble is going to be. I came round here expecting to find the police in possession of the place.'

His host was startled – alarmed. If the police came and he was taken to the station – and searched!

'Just wait one moment,' said Hermann. 'Sit here!'

Without a word of explanation he went out through the door and closed it behind him. He went down the kitchen stairs, and turned into the dark, narrow passage which led to the wine cellar. The door was locked, but the key was in his pocket. He entered, switching on the electric light which dangled between the bins. The cellar was empty!

Hermann gasped.

There was the chair, the leather thongs, with which he had bound the drugged and helpless Gordon, lay around in confusion, as though they had been thrown hastily away; but there was no sign of Gordon Bray.

He made a careful examination of the cellar. The young man might have escaped and be in hiding; but he searched without result. The cellar was too small for a man to conceal himself, and the bins offered very little shadow to any man who might seek concealment.

He came back to the chair and looked at it, and something on the ground attracted his attention, and he stooped down and looked.

At first he thought the man had helped himself to his wine, and had spilt some on the ground. The electric light did not show him what he wanted to know, and he bent down and examined the stain at close range.

He sprang up again with a cry, for that which was splashed about the ground was blood!

He ascended the stairs slowly; he was mystified and badly frightened. Who had opened the cellar door and released the prisoner? Whose blood was it that lay upon the ground and sprinkled the chair?

'What is the matter?' asked Leete, as his host re-entered the dining room.

'It was a joke,' stammered the other. He was shaking, for twice today had the fear of death been upon him.

'I took him into my study and gave him a drink, and he – he collapsed under it,' he said incoherently.

'Drugged?' said Leete accusingly.

'No, no, no! It was just a little too strong for him, that is all,' protested Hermann. 'For a joke I took him into the cellar and tied him up to a chair. I swear I meant him no harm, Leete,' he said eagerly. 'Come and look!'

The two men descended the stairs together, and Leete gazed in silence.

'What is that on the floor?' he asked.

'Blood,' said Hermann.

Leete shivered and drew back.

'I don't want to be mixed up in this,' he said.

'But I swear to you,' stormed the other, 'I know nothing about it. I left him here this morning.'

'I don't want to hear anything at all about it,' said Leete, raising a protesting hand. 'I am not in this, and know nothing of it. I most distinctly do not want to be drawn into a case of this description. Good morning!' he said hurriedly, and made a hurried and undignified exit.

Hermann was left alone in the house.

'My God!' he muttered. 'They will think I did it! The police will come here and search the place. I must wash it down.'

With feverish haste he descended to the cellar, and dragged up the chair to the daylight. He cleaned the priceless tapestry as well as he could with warm water, and set it in front of a gas stove to dry. He worked at top speed. At any moment the men of the law might call.

With great difficulty he found a pail and some water, and the paraphernalia of the charwoman, and not for the first time in his life he was engaged for ten minutes on his hands and knees in his own wine cellar removing all trace of whatever tragedy there had been.

Who could have come to the rescue? And who, having released him, would wound him? Suppose that anarchist man had come – the man he had employed to extract the secret of the combination safe from Elsie Marion? Suppose he had stolen in stealthily and discovered the prisoner? Suppose the police had already been; but no, they would not have left the house again?

In a fever of anxiety he paced the study floor, waiting for the inevitable. The evening came, but still no sign of the police. He was feeling desperately hungry; he had not eaten since breakfast, and he made a hurried toilet and went out, resolved not to return that night. He would dine at the Carlton grill. One need not dress for that, and he found himself at a little table in one of the recesses of that famous underground dining room, eating ravenously the meal which Gaston, the head waiter, put before his client.

In the next recess a merry party was dining, if he could judge from the laughter. He was too hungry to take much notice; but when the first cravings of his appetite had been assuaged he found himself with an interest in life and his surroundings. The laughter was insistent, and it grated a little on him in his present mood. Then he thought he heard his name mentioned, and half rose, straining his ears to catch what was said. He heard a voice he did not recognize.

'Of course, it was a hateful thing to do, but I just had to do it, Miss Zeberlieff.'

Hermann knitted his brows. Who was this?

'It was the artistic finish which circumstances demanded. Red ink wouldn't deceive a baby; but I'll bet it deceived him. So after I released Mr Bray...'

Hermann rose and stepped out so that he could see the diners. His sister was one, a stranger whose face he dimly remembered was another, and Gordon Bray was a notable third. They looked up and saw him staring down at them, and his sister, with a smile, caught his eye.

'You seem to have had quite an exciting day, Hermann,' she said with her sweetest smile.

CHAPTER XXII

Hermann found Leete at his club, and explained the joke. It required some explaining, and it was a long time before Leete put down the arm-length's barrier which he had erected in that moment of fancied peril.

'You shouldn't mix yourself up with that sort of thing at all, Zeberlieff,' he said disapprovingly. 'Whatever you do, keep away from the police. You can't afford to be mixed up with them – particularly if you've friends, as I have. There's my friend the Duke –'

'Oh, cut out your ducal friend for this evening!' said Hermann wearily; 'I'm sick to death of everything, and I do not think that I can stand your gospel according to Burke.'

'Have you had dinner?' asked Leete, anxious to mollify him.

Hermann laughed mirthlessly. 'I have indeed,' he said.

'Then come along and smoke; there's a lot of men up there who will be glad to talk to you. Hubbard's there, by the way,' he said.

Hermann nodded. Hubbard! Here was another proposition.

'Everybody is talking about that fellow Kerry; there's a man here from Bolt and Waudry – young Harry Bolt. Their people are in an awful funk. They say that the whole of their takings for the past two days have amounted to twenty pounds. I tell you, unless we can put a stopper to King Kerry, it is ruin for us.'

'For you individually?'

Leete hesitated.

'No,' he said. 'I am not such a fool as that. My liability is limited by shares, but I've a much bigger holding in Goulding's than is pleasant to think about at this particular moment. The only thing to do,' he went on, 'is to get at King Kerry.'

'How is his trade?'

'Bigger than ever!' said the other promptly. 'All London is flocking to his store.'

There were many gloomy faces at the Merchants' Club that night; all the great emporium proprietors were gathered together to exchange lugubrious notes.

'There's old Modelson!' said Leete, leading the way into the smoke-room. 'They say he'll file his petition next week.'

'So soon?' asked the other.

Leete nodded. 'You hardly know how hand to mouth some of these businesses are. There ain't half a dozen of us who can lay our hands upon any capital whatever, and even we should hesitate to use it just now.'

'He offered me a hundred and twenty thousand pounds for the business,' a man was saying, the centre of a little group of compassionate souls. 'I asked him a hundred and eighty. He told me I'd be glad to take a hundred before I was through, and upon my word I think he's right.'

The senior partner of Frail and Brackenbury, a tall, good-looking man, with a sharp, short, grey beard, walked over to Leete.

'I suppose he is hitting you pretty bad?' he asked.

Leete nodded.

There was no need to explain who 'he' was.

'As bad as it can be,' he said; 'but we're all in the swim. I suppose it doesn't affect you?'

'He bought me out,' said the other quietly, 'and if he hadn't I don't know that the sale would have affected our business. You see we do a line which is rather superior to that which –' He hesitated, desiring to offend none.

'That's his scheme,' said one of the club-men. 'Can't you see it? Every business he has bought spells "quality" – Q-U-A-L-I-T-Y

– throughout. Wherever a firm was associated with quality, he bought it, paying a heavy price for it. It is only we poor devils who live by cutting one another's throats that he can afford to fight. You see, we're not quality, dear old chap!'

He turned to the sad-looking Mr Bolt, of Bolt and Waudry. 'We're just big quantity and average quality. What I buy at your shop I can buy at any shop in the street. We are the people he is hitting at. We cannot say at our stores as old Frail can say,' he nodded to the grey-bearded man, 'that we have something here which you cannot buy elsewhere. If we had, why, the Yankee would have bought us up at our own price. He has gone out for quality, and he is paying money for it. And, were it just a question of common truck –'

'I'll have you to know, my dear sir,' said the sad Mr Bolt very firmly and impressively, 'that we supply nothing but the best.'

'Yes, yes, I know,' said the other with a grin; 'but it is just the ordinary best, the same best as you can get everywhere else. He can buy it too, by the ton. He is selling your best at half your prices. You've been making sixty per cent profit: he is probably making a five per cent loss at some hour of the day, and selling square on an average. I've got one piece of advice to offer to everybody in this room' – he spoke with considerable emphasis, and with the evidence of self-consciousness which comes to a man who knows that all ears are turned in his direction – 'if King Kerry has offered you money for your businesses, you go right along tomorrow morning and take what he will give you, because if this goes on much longer we're going to wear a channel in the pavement between Oxford Street and Bankruptcy Chambers.'

'I say fight!' said Leete. 'We can hold on as long as he! Don't you agree?'

He turned to Hermann Zeberlieff.

'I certainly do not,' said Zeberlieff briefly. 'You know my views; he can sell all of you out. There may be twenty ways of smashing the big "L Trust", but that is not one of them. My suggestion is that you should beat him at his own game.'

'What is that?' asked a dozen voices.

'Under-selling,' was the calm reply.

A chorus of derisive laughter met him.

'Under-selling,' said Hermann Zeberlieff. 'I assure you I am quite sane. Make a pool and under-sell him. You can do it with greater ease than you think.'

'But what about the shareholders?' asked a voice. 'What about dividends? How are we going to explain at the end of the half year that instead of a surplus we show a considerable deficit, and that we may have to issue debenture stock? Do you think shareholders are going to stand that?'

'No, no, no!' – agreement with this view came from various corners of the room.

'They've got to stand something,' said Hermann with a smile. 'Looking at it from a purely outsider's point of view, I can't see how they'll get dividends anyway. The suggestion that I was going to offer when you interrupted me was – ?'

A sudden silence fell upon the room, and Hermann turned to seek an explanation.

King Kerry stood in the doorway, his eyes searching the room for a face. He found it at last. It was the white-bearded Modelson who stood alone near the fireplace, his head bent upon his arm, dejected and sorrowful to see. With scarcely a glance at the others, King Kerry crossed the room and came to the old man's side.

'I want you, Mr Modelson,' he said gently.

The old man looked at him with a pathetic attempt at a smile.

'I am afraid you do!' he said apologetically.

Everybody knew that old Modelson had been the first to raise the flag of rebellion against the encroachment of the big 'L Trust' upon the sacred dominion of Oxford Street. His store stood on the next corner to that occupied by Goulding's, but long before the arrival of Kerry his had been a decaying property. Yet so long had he been established and so straight was his business record that it was natural he should have been chosen as chairman of the Federated Board.

Leete had seen the wisdom of electing him chairman. His concern was the shakiest of all and his failure which, as all men knew, was only deferred, must shake the credit of the Federation to a very damaging extent. And fail he must, and not one of the men to whom he had applied for assistance could help him. He had demanded what even his friends agreed was an exorbitant price for the business, and had been offered half. Now it seemed to the onlookers watching the two men talking earnestly by the fireplace, that the old man would surrender and take whatever he could to save his good name.

There were men in that room who hoped fervently that he would agree to the terms which Kerry imposed. Failure would break the old man's heart.

Their talk ended, and after a while Kerry shook hands and departed, leaving the old man with his head in the air and his shoulders thrown back and something like a smile on his face.

They longed to ask him what had resulted from the conference, but he was the doyen of them all, a man of rigid ideas as to the proprieties.

He saved them any trouble, however, for presently – 'Gentlemen!' he said in his rich old voice, and there was silence.

'Gentlemen, I think you are entitled to know that Mr Kerry has purchased my business.'

There was a little murmur of congratulation, not unmixed with relief. But what was the price? It was too much to expect that this old man who had been so close and uncommunicative all his life would be loquacious now; and yet, to their surprise he was.

'Mr Kerry has very handsomely paid me my full price,' he said.

'It's a climb down!' whispered Leete excitedly. 'He's going to pay –'

Hermann laughed savagely.

'Climb down, you fool!' he smiled. 'Why, he's going to make you pay for his generosity – all of you will contribute to the extra money he's giving Modelson. Don't you understand? Suppose old Modelson had failed – there would have been an outcry; an old-established firm ruined by unfair competition; a pathetic old man, white-haired and white-bearded, driven to the workhouse after a life spent in honourable toil. It would have made him unpopular, set the tide of public opinion against him, and possibly upset all his plans. You don't know King Kerry!'

'Anyway, I'm going to him tomorrow with my old offer,' said Leete stubbornly.

'What did he agree to pay before?' asked Zeberlieff.

'Three-quarters of a million,' replied the other.

Hermann nodded.

'He'll offer you exactly a hundred thousand less than that,' he said.

Well might he boast that he knew Kerry, for when, on the following morning, supremely confident, Leete elbowed his way through the gaping crowd that was staring through the window of the Jewel House and came to Kerry's presence, the offer 'The King' made him was exactly the sum that Hermann had prophesied.

Nor was Leete the only man who mistook the generosity of the other, nor the only one to be painfully undeceived.

CHAPTER XXIII

Elsie Marion was a busy girl and a happy one. The green on the map was spreading. She called them the 'marks of conquest', and took a pride in their extension. Then came the day of days when the papers were filled with the colossal deal which King Kerry had carried through – the purchase of Lord George Fallington's enormous estate. Lord Fallington was a millionaire peer, who derived an enormous income from ground rents in the very heart of the West End of London. He may have been urged to the action he took by the fear of new punitive legislation against landowners, and there certainly was justification for his fear, for at the time the government in power was the famous Jagger-Shubert Coalition which, with its huge democratic measures to be provided for out of revenue and its extraordinary demands in the matter of the navy (a rare combination in any government), was framing its estimate with an avaricious eye upon the land.

Whatever was the cause, Lord Fallington sold out, and when, following that event Bilsbury's fell into the hands of the Trust, the battle was half won.

One day Kerry came into the office hurriedly, and there was a look on his face which the girl had never seen before. He closed the door behind him without a word, and crossed the room to the steel door which opened into the front office, that bemirrored apartment in which stood the great safe of the Trust.

She looked up astonished as the steel door clanged behind him.

Only once since she had entered his employ had he passed that door, and she had accompanied him, standing with her back to the safe at his request whilst he manipulated the combination lock.

He was gone ten minutes, and when he returned he carried in his hand a small envelope. He stood in the centre of the room, lit a match, and applied it to one corner of the letter. He put his foot on the ashes as they fell upon the square of linoleum and crushed them to powder. This done he uttered a sigh of infinite relief, and smiled at the girl's evident concern.

'Thus perish all traitors!' quoth he gaily. 'There was something in that envelope which I very much wanted to destroy.'

'I gathered that,' she laughed.

He walked over to her desk.

'You're getting snowed under,' he said. 'I'll buy you one of those talking machines, and you can dictate your replies. There's room in the commissionaire's office for a typist.'

She shook her head. 'There isn't enough work, really,' she protested.

He made no further allusion to the burnt envelope. She might speculate (as she did) upon the contents: what precious secret was here hidden, what urgency dictated its destruction. There were such secret places in this unknown world into which she had entered in the joyous spirit of exploration – thick jungles where lurked the beast of prey waiting to spring, dark woods above and morasses beneath her feet, pitfalls cunningly dug and traps ingeniously laid.

Kerry was an experienced hunter. He skirted trap and fall, walked warily always, with an eye to dangers of the tall grasses, and never penetrated the dim channels of his profession without being sure that every weapon in his arsenal was in good working order and to hand.

Notes, letters, telegrams came every minute of the day. Mysterious and brief epistles unintelligible to her, full of meaning to him. The telephone bell would ring: 'Yes!' he would reply, or 'No!' and hang up the receiver. What was his objective in this campaign of his? The newspapers were asking, his friends were asking, his enemies were demanding an answer to that question. Why was he buying up unfashionable Tottenham Court Road and Lambeth Walk and a score of other places which just stood on the fringe of the shopping centre of London?

'He is acting,' said one critic, 'as though he expected shopping London to shift from the circle – the centre of which is halfway along Regent Street to – ?'

Here the critic must pause irresolutely.

'To whither?'

It seemed that Kerry anticipated not so much the shifting of the centre, as the extension of the circle. A sanguine man if he imagined that his operations and the operations of his syndicate would so increase the prosperity of London that he would double the shopping area of fashionable London.

There was a Mr Biglow Holden, a pompous, self-important man who had earned a fortune as a designer of semi-important buildings, who wrote a very learned article in the *Building Mail*. It was filled with statistical tables (printed in small type) showing the growth of London in relation to population, and it proved conclusively that Mr King Kerry must wait some three hundred and fifty years before his dream materialized.

Gordon Bray, who happened to be engaged in Mr Holden's office, typed the article for his employer, and heartily disagreed with every conclusion, every split infinitive and error of taste and grammar that it contained.

Holden asked him his opinion of the article, and the young man in his honesty hesitated before replying.

'I suppose you think you could do it better?' said Mr Biglow Holden, in his heavy jocular style.

'I think I could,' replied Gordon innocently.

Mr Holden glowered at him.

'You're getting a swelled head, Bray!' he said, warningly. 'This isn't the office for young fellows with swelled heads, remember that.'

King Kerry read the article and frowned. He had a very good reason for frowning. He sent for Mr Holden, and, for one who had so openly despised 'Yankee acumen', to quote his own phrase, he obeyed the summons with considerable alacrity.

'So you think my scheme is all wrong?' asked the millionaire.

'I think your judgement is at fault,' said Mr Holden with an ingratiating smile.

'Does everybody think that?'

'Everybody except my draughtsman,' smiled Mr Holden again.

It was intended to be a politely crushing answer, and to convey the fact that only the more inexperienced and menial departments of architecture would be found ranged on the side of the amateur designer.

'Your draughtsman?' Kerry frowned again. 'I have an idea we know him.' He turned to the girl.

'Mr Bray is the gentleman, I think,' said Elsie.

'You see,' explained Holden hurriedly, 'his ideas are rather fantastic. He's a product of what I might term the Evening Class – all theory and half-digested knowledge. He has an idea that you can jump into the middle of London and push it out.'

'Humph!' said King Kerry thoughtfully – then – 'And you would not advise me to rebuild – let us say, Tottenham Court Road?'

The architect hesitated.

'No,' he said – and what else could he say in the face of his article?

'I'm sorry,' said King Kerry shortly, 'for I was going to ask you to submit designs – but naturally I cannot give the work to a man without enthusiasm.'

'Of course there might be something I haven't understood about your –'

Kerry shook his head.

'I think you understand all that I wish anybody to understand,' he said, and saw the discomfited Mr Holden to the door.

Gordon Bray stood at the broad draughtsman's table employing his compasses and his rulers to the front elevation of a particularly hideous building which Mr Holden was calling into being.

He was in a state of depression. The goal was very far distant to him. He could never marry now until he had secured a position in the world. His self-respect would not allow him to share the fortune of the woman he loved. So far he was ignorant of the provisions of her father's will, but enlightenment on that question would not have changed the outlook. A man loves a woman best when he can bring gifts in his hands: it is unnatural to come not only empty-handed but with hands to be filled. He had all the pride and sensitiveness of youth. The whisper of the phrase 'fortune hunter' was sufficient to turn him hot and cold, though it might bear no relationship to him and had never been intended to apply. Though, possibly, only three persons in London knew of his love, he thought his secret was common property, and it was a maddening thought that perhaps there were people who spoke disparagingly or sneeringly of his beautiful lady for her graciousness to a penniless draughtsman.

He had had wild thoughts of ending the situation. It was unfair to her. He would write a letter and go away to Canada, and perhaps come back some day a wealthy man to find her heart still free.

Many young men have the same heroic thought and lack the ready cash necessary to make the change. He at any rate was in this position, and had grown savage in the realization when Holden's bell summoned him.

Holden was very red in the face, and very angry. His fat cheeks were puffed out and his round eyes stared comically – but he had no desire to amuse anybody.

His stare was almost terrifying as Gordon entered.

'I've just seen that damned Yankee!' he said.

'Which damned Yankee?' demanded the young man. In his own distress of mind he forgot to be impressed by his employer.

'There's only one,' growled Mr Holden. 'He's full of silly-ass ideas about building... sent for me to insult me... thinks he knows... here, take this letter to him!'

He handed a sealed envelope across the table with a malicious grin.

'You seem to have friends in that office,' he went on, and fished in the drawer of his desk for a cheque book. 'I'm beginning to understand now how Kerry came to buy that Borough property that my client wanted!'

He referred to a transaction which was a month old, but the memory of which still rankled.

'What do you mean?' asked the young man, raising his voice.

'Never mind what I mean,' said Mr Holden darkly; 'and don't shout at me, Gordon!' he snorted the last word. 'Here's your cheque for a month's salary. Deliver the letter and you needn't come back: perhaps Mr Kerry will engage you as his architect – you've passed all the examinations, I understand.'

Gordon picked up the cheque slowly. 'Do you mean that I am dismissed?'

'I mean,' said Mr Holden, 'that you're too clever for this office.'

It was with a heavy heart that the young man entered Kerry's office. Elsie was not there, and Kerry received him alone, read the letter in silence, then tore up a letter he was writing himself.

'Do you know the contents of this?' Mr Kerry held up Holden's epistle.

'No, Mr Kerry.'

'I thought you didn't,' said the big man with a smile, 'otherwise you mightn't have brought it. I'll read it to you –'

DEAR SIR, – Since you do not require expert advice and may need assistance to rebuild London! ('He's put a note of exclamation there,' said Kerry with a twinkle in his eye), I send you along my draughtsman, who makes up in enthusiasm all he lacks in experience. I have no further use for him.
Yours faithfully,

BIGLOW HOLDEN.

Gordon's face was crimson.

'How dare he!' he cried.

'Dare he?' Kerry's eyebrows rose. 'Goodness gracious! – as you English say – he's given you the finest testimonial I have ever had with a young man. I gather you're sacked?'

Gordon nodded.

'Excellent!' said the other. 'Now you go along to an office I have just taken in St. James's Street and furnish it – I give you carte blanche – as a surveyor's office should be furnished. And if anybody asks who you are, you must say: "I am the architect of the big L Trust," and,' he added solemnly, 'they will probably take their hats off to you.'

'But, seriously, Mr Kerry?' protested the laughing Gordon.

'Never more serious. Go along and design something.'

Gordon Bray was transfixed, hypnotized – he couldn't grasp the meaning of it all.

'Design me,' said Kerry, wrinkling his brow in thought, 'a public square set around with buildings, shops, and public offices. Let the square be exactly half the length of Regent Street from side to side.'

With a curt nod he dismissed the dazed youth.

CHAPTER XXIV

'That's a weird contrivance you have, Zeberlieff!'

Martin Hubbard, immaculately dressed, stood looking over the shoulder of his unconscious friend.

Hermann swung round with an oath. 'How did you get in?' he asked roughly.

'Through the door. I was coming in when your man was going out to the post.'

Hermann got up from the table at which he had been experimenting.

'Come down into the dining room,' he said shortly. 'I hate people sneaking in behind me: it gives me the creeps!'

'But,' said the other humorously, 'you don't mind your future brother-in-law, surely' – a remark which restored the good humour of the other, for he chuckled as he led the way downstairs.

'Future brother-in-law – yes,' he said.

'What was that funny old machine?' persisted Hubbard. 'Never knew you were a dabbler in science. You're quite a Louis the Fourteenth with your passion for applied mechanics.'

'It is an invention sent to me by a man,' said Hermann carelessly; 'did you notice it very closely?'

Hubbard shook his head.

'Only what looked like an alarm clock and a bit of wadding and some stuff that looked like a cinematograph film.'

'It's a new kind of – er – cinema projector,' explained Zeberlieff readily. 'It's automatic – wakes you up with pictures on the ceiling.'

'And what were the matches for?'

'Matches!' Zeberlieff eyed him narrowly. 'There were no matches.'

'I must have been mistaken.' Hubbard was not sufficiently interested to pursue the subject, and went on: 'I suppose you know I've come by appointment?'

'The devil you have?'

'You told me to call,' said the other a little irritated, 'with the idea of meeting your sister.'

'Did I?' Hermann favoured him with a thoughtful stare. 'So I did – that's rather awkward for both of us, because she won't see you.'

'Won't see me?'

The chagrin and the wounded pride in the man's voice was laughable.

'She won't see you – she won't see me, that is all; here's a letter, if it will interest!'

Mr Hubbard opened the grey note slowly, and read –

> *I cannot receive you nor your beautiful friend. If you come any-where near me I send for the police. – V.*

'What do you think of that?' asked the calm Hermann.

'It's monstrous!' gasped Hubbard. 'How dare she – she –'

'Call you beautiful? Oh, well, there's every excuse for her,' soothed Hermann. 'And really I'm not worrying now.'

'Listen!' said Mr Hubbard, 'I want to ask you something. What chance have I of raising a monkey?'

'All depends upon the care you give it,' replied Hermann, wilfully dense. 'In this climate –'

'I want to borrow five hundred pounds,' said Mr Hubbard more explicitly.

'Borrow it, by all means!' suggested Zeberlieff unmoved.

'Could you let me have it?'

Hermann considered.

'No,' he said, 'I could not. Of course,' he went on, 'if I thought there was any chance of your marrying my sister I would hang little wads of banknotes round your throat: but I fancy your chance is down around the zero mark.'

'In fact,' said the indignant Hubbard, 'you think I am no more use to you.'

'What a mind you have!' admired Hermann. 'You grasp these things so quickly.'

Martin Hubbard bit at his golden moustache.

'Suppose I went to your sister and told her your proposition,' he suggested.

'She would be bored to tears,' replied Hermann with his smile. 'You see, I've already told her. The fact is, Hubbard, she's in love with a young man, the son of poor but honest parents. It's working out rather like a story. I'm afraid she's going to marry him. The only hope for you is that you and she should be cast ashore on some desert island. At the end of five years you might like one another – and anyway, the marriage would be convenient for the sake of the proprieties. If you could arrange for the shipwreck, and could guarantee that only you and she would be saved, I might fix up the passage and the island.'

He was in his most flippant mood, but his good humour touched no responsive chord in the breast of Mr Hubbard.

'It is all very well for you,' he said miserably; 'you're a jolly rich man – but I'm broke to the wide world.'

'As I shall be next week,' said Hermann cheerfully. 'Another week's trading like last week, and Goulding's goes to the devil.'

'Are you in it?' asked the interested Mr Hubbard.

'Up to the neck,' said Hermann shortly. 'Leete got me in to the extent of two hundred thousand. I've lost another two hundred thousand in the slump in American rails. What are you envying me for, you silly ass?'

'When is this cut-throat sale going to stop?' demanded Hubbard.

Hermann shook his head.

'He has a warehouse filled with stuff in South London – a year's supply. Otherwise we could have brought pressure to bear upon the manufacturers. But he bought his stock in advance, and he's selling exactly six times the amount of goods that any other house in Oxford Street has sold in its biggest sale week – and he's losing practically nothing. There's a big margin of profit on soft goods. He can sell at cost price and ruin the other stores. So long as he's got the goods to sell, he'll sell 'em, and, as I say, his warehouses in South London are chock-full.'

'What about that five hundred?' asked Hubbard abruptly.

'Not here, my child,' said Hermann. 'When you come down to fifty, I'll be listening to you – because I think you might be worth fifty – and besides, you're on the Federated board, and I can stop it from your director's fees.'

Five minutes later he was back in his study, working at his little machine. He took the precaution this time to lock the door.

It was now a month since the beginning of the Kerry sale, and the queues so far from diminishing had increased. As every week passed and the fame of the Kerry bargain extended, the all-night shopping house attracted even greater numbers than in the day of its novelty. Then Modelson's fell into the Kerry combination, and promptly changed its name and its methods. Hastily remodelled on the lines of the original store, it ended the rush on Kerry's.

'The same price, the same system, the same name,' said a flamboyant advertisement announcing the change. It gave Kerry's a breathing space; but the queues came back, only now there were two – one to Kerry's, and the other to what had been Modelson's. Between the two stores, a howling desert, with customers as scarce as December flies, was Goulding's – Goulding's, the once busy hive of industry, now almost deserted.

In vain were prices reduced, in vain were enticing bargains placed in the window. Customers went after them, it is true, but discovered that they were already sold. 'The only model of that kind we have in stock, madam!' and came away wrathful at the trick which had been played upon them, refusing to see 'something else just as good'.

Kerry had to undergo the trial of a press campaign. A savage attack on his methods appeared in a weekly journal. Scarcely was the paper in print and on the street, when the 'King's' own journal, the *Evening Herald*, replied. It was not a polite reply. It was personal and overpoweringly informative. It gave the relationship of the attacking weekly with Leete, printed a list of shareholders and a list of Leete's directorships. Said unpleasant things about the editor of the weekly, and concluded with a promise of revelations concerning 'a moving spirit in this conspiracy who hatches in Park Lane the plots which are executed in Whitechapel'.

'Stop it!' was Hermann Zeberlieff's order, and the next issue of the *Weekly Discovery* was notable for its dignified silence on the subject of Kerry and his ways.

Nothing helped Goulding's. A window dressed with enticing bargains produced a notice on the next window (which happened to be Kerry's end show window) –

'All the "bargains" there can be purchased in this Store at exactly half the price demanded by our competitor.'

The hand pointed remorselessly to Goulding's last hope.

Manufacturers were wavering. They could afford to be sympathetic with the affected houses because, for the moment, they were not being called upon to supply Kerry.

Kerry paid cash, and when another journal hinted that he was able to sell so cheaply only because the articles he supplied were made by sweated labour, he published a list of the manufacturers, and thus forced them to take action for libel.

Then the *Daily Courier* took a hand in support of Kerry baiting, but here the *Evening Herald* was careful and mild, for the *Courier* is a powerful daily.

'It has been asked,' said the *Herald*, 'what association there is between the sale in Oxford Street and Mr Kerry's operations in land. The answer may be supplied in a few words. Mr Kerry desires to beautify London, and at the same time secure a modest return from investment in land. To secure both ends it is necessary that certain stores fall into his hands. He has offered an equitable price and has received exorbitant demands. It is now his business to weaken opposition, and this he intends doing.' (Here followed a list of the properties he had offered to buy; the prices he had tendered; the profits and dividends paid by the various concerns, and the prices demanded.) 'Thus it will be seen,' the journal continued, 'that the prices tendered were reasonable. We are authorized to say that though the conditions have changed, Mr King Kerry is willing to pay the sums he originally tendered for these properties – this offer being open till midday tomorrow.'

Leete came to Hermann with the newspaper still wet from the press, and he was pardonably excited.

'Look here, Zeberlieff,' he said, 'I'm selling!'

Hermann took the paper and read.

'I'm selling before a worse thing happens,' Leete went on.

Hermann's smile was one of quiet contempt. 'If you must sell – sell to me,' he said.

'To you?'

'Why not? I hold a big block of shares, and you or your nominees hold the rest.'

'And you'll give Kerry's price?'

'Yes.'

Leete looked at the other.

'It's a bargain,' he said. 'I'm glad to be rid of it.'

'You may have lost a million,' said Hermann, and went back to his study.

Elsie Marion had gone home from her office with a headache, with strict injunction from King Kerry not to return whilst any vestige of the malady remained. She had reached her flat a little after twelve, and with the comfort of a cup of tea and an aspirin, had lain down on her bed with the intention of rising at two to have a lunch. When she awoke it was nearly dark, and she came to consciousness with that feeling of panic which is born of a sense of wasted time and a complete ignorance of the amount of time so wasted. She looked at her watch. It was nearly nine o'clock. She rose and dined – her patient maid had a chop ready for her by the time she had dressed.

It was ten o'clock before she had finished dinner. Her headache had gone, and she felt immensely energetic. There was some work at the office which she would bring away with her – she never liked working at the office at night. King Kerry had a trick of working at unconscionable hours, and she felt that on these occasions he liked to be alone.

She indulged in the luxury of a taxi to the office, and passing the guard and the commissionaire in his little box, she unlocked the office door and went in. She bundled her work together and put it in her bag. Then she noticed a note on King Kerry's desk written in pencil and addressed to her.

I have gone to the warehouse: come down if you are feeling fit. – K. K.

'When did Mr Kerry go out?' she asked the commissionaire.

The man shook his head.

'I didn't come on duty till nine, miss,' he said. 'He hasn't been here since then.'

It might have been written early in the afternoon; but he would have been back and destroyed it if that were so.

She was feeling very much awake and rested. The spin over the water to the big riverside warehouse would do her good. Another taxi was requisitioned, and deposited her in the great courtyard of Kerry's Storage. It was formed of three tall buildings so arranged to form the three sides of a square. The ends of two of the stores were flush with the edge of the wharf, and the third was pierced with a great gateway through which laden wagons were coming and going.

It was a scene of extraordinary bustle and activity. The windows blazed with lights, for a large number of workmen were now employed in unpacking and sorting the goods prior to delivery in Oxford Street.

'Mr Kerry is somewhere in the building, I think, miss,' said the timekeeper, 'but nobody has seen him during the past hour.'

'Never mind!' said the girl. 'I will find him presently!'

She had the entrée to all the departments and passed an amusing half-hour watching the men and girls at work. The great packing-cases and baskets came to the first floor and were stripped of their lids, their zinc covers expeditiously and deftly cut, and the contents thrown upon a broad sorting table. Here they were counted and laid on an endless belt and conveyed to the next floor. Here they were counted again and deposited in huge zinc-lined presses to await the requisitions from Oxford Street.

Hundreds of cases were waiting in the big storage space on the ground floor and in the basement. Here, too, were kept huge quantities of stuffs, satins, cottons, silks, delaines and linens.

'Goods are arriving every day, miss,' said one of the foremen. 'These' – he indicated a chaos of yellow and wood cases and dull brown bales – 'will be here a month before we handle 'em.'

'I suppose they are coming from the manufacturers all the time?' she asked.

'All the time – there's a package just arrived,' he pointed to a man in the leather apron of the carrier, a box on his shoulder.

'What would that be?' asked Elsie.

'Looks like gloves – they come in those small cases.'

She waited till the package had been deposited on the weigh-bridge just inside the entrance gate, and examined it. 'Yes, miss, "Gants Cracroix – Lyons",' he read.

The carter took his delivery sheet and made his way out of the building and a man caught the case with a practised hand and sent it sliding down the slipway.

'Are you learning something?'

She heard the deep, rich note of King Kerry, and turned, smiling.

'Headache better?' he asked.

'Quite all right, I feel awfully guilty – I've only just got up.'

He led the way down to the end of the warehouse where the men were working with that fervour which is equally induced by piecework and the proximity of the employer.

'There's a case of wonderful lace being unpacked over there,' he said; 'you ought to see it.'

'I should love to!' she said, and picked her way through the cases to where a number of women were lifting the narrow trays from the big cabinet.

In her eagerness she failed to notice a rope that lay on the ground: her toe caught, and she went sprawling and would have injured herself but for her presence of mind to catch at the edges of a small case that lay in her path.

Her arms took the strain, and her face just touched the top of the case.

'My God, she's hurt!' King Kerry leapt nimbly over the packages toward her. He was justified in his mistake, for she lay for some time with her head on the box where she had fallen.

But it was a smiling face she turned to him as she rose unassisted to her feet.

'Are you sure you aren't hurt?' he asked.

She shook her head.

A man came to move the little packing-case upon which she had rested. It was the case of gloves which she had seen arrive.

'Don't touch that, please!' she said quickly.

'What is it?'

King Kerry looked at her in amazement.

'Ask the men to lift that case on to the wharf,' she said, 'and tell them to be very careful with it.' Wonderingly, he turned to give the order, and followed the men to the wharf without.

'Whatever is wrong?' he asked.

'I don't know quite,' she said, 'but put your ear to that box, and listen!'

He obeyed, and rose up with a frown. He put his nose to the box, and sniffed.

'Open the box carefully!' he said.

For he heard the loud tick-tick-tick, as plainly as she.

'It may be an infernal machine,' she said; but he shook his head.

'I think I know what it is,' he said quietly.

Under a powerful arc light, lowered from its standard to afford a better view, the box was opened. On the top was a layer of paper carefully folded, but under that the case seemed to be packed tightly with shavings of some transparent material.

'Celluloid!' said King Kerry briefly, 'an old cinema film cut up in short lengths.'

They cleared this out before they came to the machine itself.

It was screwed to the bottom of the case, and enclosed in a wicker-work cage of flimsy material. It consisted of a clock, a small electric battery, and few shavings.

'Set for two o'clock,' said King Kerry; 'the hour our men finish. The alarm key soldered to a piece of metal so that when the alarm goes off the strip of metal turns with the key, a contact is made, and a spark sets the celluloid ablaze – highly ingenious! I'll show you how it is done!' He carried the machine to the edge of the water, where there was no danger of the fire spreading, placed it upon a steel plate, and buried the machine in the celluloid shavings after manipulating the alarm hand.

They waited, and in a minute they heard the whirr of the alarm as it spun; then there was a tiny flicker of light amongst the celluloid shavings, a sudden roar of flame, and the wharf was illuminated with a tongue of fire that leapt up from the blazing film.

They watched it in silence until it died down to the molten red of something which had been a clock.

'I could have kept that clock for evidence,' said King Kerry, 'but he will have covered his tracks. How can I thank you, Elsie?' he asked. He turned and faced her; they stood in the shadow of a great stack of cases piled in the centre of the wharf.

'Thank me?' she said tremulously. 'Why, it is I who have to thank you.'

He laid both his hands on her shoulders and looked down into her face. She met his gaze fearlessly.

'Once there was a girl like you,' he said softly, 'and I loved her as a man may love a child – too young to be shadowed with the thing we men call love. And the thing I loved was a husk – just an outward mask, and when she lifted the mask it nearly killed me. And here is Elsie Marion with the face and laughing eyes – and the heart of a woman behind the face, and the brain of a comrade behind the eyes –'

He dropped his hands suddenly, and he fell forward as though weighted with infinite weariness.

'What is the matter?' she asked in alarm.

'Nothing!' his voice was hard. 'Only I wish I hadn't been a fool – once.'

She waited with a beating heart; she knew something dreadful was coming.

'I am married to the worst woman in the world. God help me!' he said brokenly.

* * * * *

'What the dickens do you want to go to the City for?' grumbled John Leete, 'at this hour?'

He looked at his watch. It wanted a quarter to two o'clock in the morning, and the club was an inviting place, for Leete was an inveterate gossip.

'I love the City at this hour,' said Hermann calmly. 'Let us come along and see the enemy's stronghold.'

'Fat lot of good that will do,' growled Leete.

'Sometimes your vulgarity appals me,' said Zeberlieff with a little smile, 'and I think of all vulgarity there is none quite so hopelessly appalling as the English variety.'

His car was waiting outside, and Leete, still grumbling, allowed himself to be led to its interior.

'It is better to breathe good fresh air than fill your lungs with the poison of a beastly smoke-room,' he said as the car went its noiseless way eastward.

Mr Leete made a noise of dissent. 'I never do things that are unnecessary,' he said.

'It is necessary to propitiate the new proprietor of Goulding's,' said Hermann softly.

Leete grinned in the darkness. He regarded himself as 'well out' of that concern. Let Zeberlieff make his million and welcome – if he could.

'I'll send you the papers tomorrow,' he said as a thought struck him. 'By the way, you might give me a line tonight to the effect that you agree –'

'Certainly!' said the other easily. He stopped the car in King William Street. 'Walk across London Bridge and pay homage to the genius of King Kerry,' he said.

Leete grunted disrespectfully, and let himself down from the car. 'Well?'

They had stopped in one of the stone recesses on the bridge, and were gazing intently across the river. A passing policeman, walking on noiseless soles, eyed them, and stopped at Hermann's friendly nod.

'I suppose, constable, that big building with the lights is Mr Kerry's famous warehouse?'

'Yes, sir,' said the man, stretching himself from the belt upward in the manner of policemen, 'that is the King of London's magazine, so to speak.'

A ghost of a smile nickered over the features of Zeberlieff. 'A rare fright he gave my mate tonight,' the policeman went on, 'he was on the bridge between ten and eleven and suddenly the whole of the wharf seemed burning.'

'Burning?' Zeberlieff's voice expressed interest.

'It was only a packing case – something was wrong with it, and Mr Kerry himself touched it off. My mate is serving a summons on him tomorrow; it's against the law to light bonfires on a wharf.'

'So he found something was wrong with it and touched it off, did he?' repeated Hermann, without a tremor of voice. 'How like Kerry to be there when something was wrong.' He offered the constable a tip, and was a little surprised when it was courteously refused.

'Queer people, these City police,' said Leete.

'Not so queer as Kingy,' said the other cryptically.

Not a word was spoken as they drove back westward.

Nearing Piccadilly, Leete seized the opportunity to make his bargain solid.

'Come in, and we'll fix up that agreement,' he said as the car stopped, and he stepped heavily to the pavement.

'Which agreement?' asked Hermann coolly.

'The sale of Goulding's,' said the other.

He caught the flash of Zeberlieff's white teeth as he smiled. 'Don't be silly!' he said good-naturedly. 'I was joking.'

To say that Leete was staggered is to express in a relatively mild phrase a most tremendous emotion.

'But – but –' he stammered.

'Good night!' said Hermann as he slammed the door of the car and pressed the electric signal to his driver.

He left Mr Leete, a helpless figure, standing on the kerb, and looking stupidly after the fast-vanishing car.

CHAPTER XXV

The secret was out. London was amazed and staggered. It went about its several avocations, its head whizzing with figures. The Press devoted columns to the extraordinary story.

'King Kerry has bought London!' ran a flaming headline across a whole page of the *Examiner*.

It was an excusable exaggeration. If he had not bought London he had dug into the heart of it. He had belted it with a broad belt of business areas.

London was to be reshaped. He had laid his plans with extraordinary genius, avoiding the Crown property as being unpurchasable, and the adamantine ground landlord's domain. Here was the plan admirably summarized in the columns of the *Evening Herald*, which spoke with authority –

> *The greater portion of the property situated between the southern end of Portland Place on the north, Vigo Street on the south, Bond Street on the west, and Dean Street on the east, was to be demolished, and in its place was to be established a great Central Square to be known as The Imperial Place. The site to be presented to the nation save the building sites which ran on the four sides of the Square.*
>
> *A new residential suburb consisting of houses ranging from one hundred pounds to two hundred pounds per annum to be established in Lambeth on the south bank of the river, between Blackfriars and Westminster, and between Blackfriars and Southwark.*
>
> *(This would entail the complete demolition of all slum property between the river and the crossroads known as the Elephant and Castle.)*

'I intend,' said Kerry in an interview, 'to create on the south side of the river a new Champs Élysées. Between Westminster Bridge Road and Waterloo Road I shall erect a noble avenue flanked by the houses of the wealthy. It will run almost to the water's edge, and will terminate at either end in a triumphal arch which shall be worthy to rank with the Arc de Triomphe.'

It was to an interested crowd of reporters which had gathered in his office.

'What will you do with the people you displace, Mr Kerry?' asked one of the journalists. 'I refer, of course, to the slum people who are entitled, if they possibly can, to live near their places of livelihood.'

'I have provided for that,' said Mr Kerry. 'I recognize the necessity of making very ample provision in that respect. I shall create my own slums,' he smiled. 'It is a hateful word, and it is only one which I employ to designate a congested area occupied by the poor. I shall not, of course, attempt to make any provisions for the mendicant, the semi-mendicant, or for what I might term the casual itinerant class. My idea of a poor family is one in which the combined efforts of all its adult members do not produce enough money to provide the necessities of life. For these at intervals in my residential belt, I am erecting co-operative flats.'

He took from a large portfolio a series of drawings, and laid them on the table before the crowding pressmen.

'You will see,' he said, 'that in point of design we have copied the elevation of some of the most beautiful hotels in London. Indeed, I think we may say that we have gone beyond that. These buildings will be absolutely complete in themselves. Tenants will only be admitted who agree to the co-operative system. Stores providing every commodity will be found in the building itself. There will be baths, gymnasia, playgrounds, a hospital, a crèche, and a free library. Each building,' he said briefly, 'will be self-governed, will contain its doctor, its dentist, and its trained nurses, all of whom will be at the disposal of the citizens of this little community free of all charge.

'A system of elevators will make the highest floor as accessible as the lowest – indeed, the highest rents will be for the top floors. All the employees in the community will be subject to the discipline of a committee which will be elected by the tenants themselves. Although we shall provide fireplaces, the whole of the building will be run on a system of central heating; hot water and electric light will be included in the rent, and we hope to give every family six thousand cubic feet of space. Each building,' he concluded, 'will have accommodation for a thousand families.'

'What is your object, Mr Kerry,' asked a curious reporter, 'in buying so much valuable property in the centre of the West End and then destroying it? Isn't it so much money thrown away?'

Kerry shook his head.

'What happens,' he asked, 'when a policeman rides his horse into the centre of a crowd? Is it not a fact that the crowd swells out and covers almost a third as much space as before? At any rate, this is a fact: that a thousand square feet stolen from the heart of London means that ten thousand feet more are occupied on its outskirts. Briefly,' he went on, 'in the heart of London you are restricted as to space. There are many businesses which would willingly and gladly extend their present premises to twice the size they at present occupy but for the prohibitive cost, and very often the absolute impossibility of securing adjacent premises renders this impossible. We have said "You have got to get out of this anyway," and now we have given the firms which have been disturbed – and which generally are now mine,' he said with a smile, 'an opportunity of taking space adequate to their needs. People are coming to the centre to shop – do not doubt that – this is the rule of all towns. We merely extend the boundaries of the exclusive shopping district and give an incentive to private enterprises to assist us in our work of beautifying London.

'I am satisfied as to this,' he said. 'That we shall have the satisfaction of knowing that we shall enrich thousands and impoverish none by what we have done. You may now understand my action in regard to my sales. It was necessary. Tack and Brighten, Modelson and Goulding, they abutted into the square of my dreams; they are now my exclusive property. I bought Goulding's this morning,' he said with a little twitch of his mouth at the recollection of an agitated and almost tearful Mr Leete, making his unconditional surrender.

'My sale will continue until the end of the year, until, in fact, I am ready to pull down and start rebuilding. And in the meantime,' he added, 'I have guaranteed the dividends of all the firms which I have not purchased, but which are directly affected as a result of my action.'

Here was enough for London to discuss; sufficient to set heads shaking and nodding and tongues wagging from one end of London to the other. Here began, too, the London land boom which was the feature of the memorable year. It was found that King Kerry had acquired great blocks of property here and there. Sometimes they comprised whole streets, but he had left enough for the land speculator to build his fortunes upon. Automatically, the value of land rose in certain districts by one hundred and two hundred per cent, and it is said, though there is little evidence to support the fact, that in one week King Kerry himself, on behalf of his syndicate, made a profit of over a million pounds from the sale of land which he had recently included in his purchases, but for which he himself had no immediate use.

It is a fact that when his plan became generally known he received the heartiest co-operation from the Government, and, though he might not touch Crown freehold, every facility was given to him to further his scheme.

He had planned a garden city to extend in an unbroken line from Southwark to Rotherhithe and on to Deptford – a new City Beautiful, rising out of the dust of squalid, insanitary cottages and jerry-built dwellings. His plan was given in detail in an issue of the *Evening Herald*, which attained a circulation limited only by the capacity of its output.

It was obvious now that money had flowed like water into London, and that it was not alone the six men who had set out to accomplish so much who had assisted in the fulfilment of King Kerry's plans, but all the great insurance companies of America, all the big railways, all the great industrial concerns had contributed largely.

It was computed by a financial authority that the big 'L Trust' had incurred liabilities (and presumably they were in a position to meet those liabilities) amounting to eighty million pounds. Somebody asked King Kerry if this were so.

'I will tell you,' he answered good-humouredly, 'after I have counted the change in my pocket.'

King Kerry rented a little house in Cadogan Square. It is characteristic of the man that he lived on the property of others. It is also remarkable that he – the owner of millions – should have hired the house furnished, but his action may be explained by his favourite dictum, 'Never buy what you don't want, and never hire what you need.'

He did not want either the house or furniture. The house was situated in a region beyond the scope of his speculations.

Here, with an elderly housekeeper to attend to him during the few hours he was at home, he secured the quiet that was necessary to him. The house was not taken in his name, and none of the people who dwelt in the Square had the slightest idea of the identity of the tenant who usually returned in the middle of the night and afforded them no greater opportunity for recognition than the few seconds it took him to step from his front door into his closed car.

Even Elsie Marion, who knew the whereabouts of the house, had never been there, nor addressed him there. So that when he sat at his frugal dinner, and his elderly servitor brought a message that a gentleman wished to see Mr Kerry, he was pardonably annoyed.

'I told him there wasn't any such person living here, sir,' said the housekeeper, who was as ignorant of her master's identity as the rest of the Square.

Possibly a reporter who had hunted him down, thought Kerry. 'Show him into the drawing room,' he said, and finished his dinner at leisure. The irritation quickly passed – after all, there was no longer any necessity for concealment. In a week's time he would be on his way to the Continent to take the rest which he felt was so necessary. All things were shaping well.

The magnates of Oxford Street had fallen, the plan for the rebuilding of London was public property; now was the time, if ever, to take things easy.

He put down his serviette, walked upstairs to the first landing and entered the little drawing room.

A man was standing by the mantelpiece with his back to Kerry, and as the 'man who bought London' closed the door he turned.

It was Hermann Zeberlieff. For the space of a minute the two faced each other, neither speaking.

'To what am I indebted?' began Kerry.

Hermann interrupted him, almost roughly. 'Let us cut all that out,' he said, 'and come right down to business.'

'I do not know that I have any business that I wish to discuss with you,' said King Kerry, quietly.

'Oh, yes, you have, Mr Kerry,' drawled Hermann, mockingly, 'you probably know that I am in a very bad place. What opportunity I had you most ruthlessly destroyed. I was in your infernal syndicate.'

'Not by my wish,' said the other. 'I did not know of it until you were in.'

'And then you took the earliest opportunity of getting me out,' said Hermann with his twisted smile. 'I'm afraid,' he went on with a show of regret, 'I'm a vain beggar – vanity was always my undoing. The temptation to let all the world know that I was figuring in this great combination was too strong. However, we won't discuss that. What I do wish you to understand is that at the present moment I have a few thousand between me and absolute beggary.'

'That is no business of mine.' King Kerry was brief; he wasted no words with his visitor.

'But it is very much a business of mine,' said Hermann quickly. 'Now, you have to assist me – you've put me into an awful mess, and you must please lend a helping hand to pull me out. You are, as I happen to know, a particularly soft-hearted man, and you would not desire to see a fellow-creature reduced to living within his income.'

There was little softness in King Kerry's face. The humour of the other, such as it was, made no appeal to him. His lips were set hard, his eyes cold and forbidding.

'I will do nothing for you,' he said. 'Nothing – nothing!'

Hermann shrugged his shoulders.

'Then I'm afraid,' he said, 'that I shall have to force you.'

'Force me?' A contemptuous smile played about the grim face of the grey-haired man.

'Force you,' repeated the other. 'You see, Mr King Kerry, you have a wife –'

'We will not discuss her,' said King Kerry harshly.

'Unfortunately, I must discuss her,' insisted Hermann. His tone was soft and gentle, almost caressing. 'You see, she has some claim on me. I feel a certain responsibility towards her, remembering the honoured name she bore before she married you, and,' he added carefully, 'before you deserted her.'

The other made no reply.

'Before you deserted her,' repeated Hermann. 'It was a peculiarly unhappy business, was it not? And I fear you did not behave with that genial courtesy, that largeness of heart, which the Press today tell me are your chief characteristics.'

'I behaved fairly to her,' said Kerry steadily. 'She tried to ruin me, even went into competition against me behind my back and used the knowledge she had secured as my wife to that end. She was an infamous woman.'

'Is,' murmured the other.

'She is, then,' said King Kerry. 'If you come to appeal in her name, you may as well appeal to this wall.'

Hermann nodded.

'But suppose I produce your wife to the admiring gaze of London; suppose I say "This person is Mrs King Kerry, the unbeloved wife of Mr King Kerry," and so-and-so and so forth?'

'That would not shake my determination,' said Kerry. 'You cannot use that lever to force me into giving you money.'

'We shall see!' said the other. He picked up his hat and favoured Kerry with a little bow and walked from the room.

King Kerry stood as if rooted to the ground long after the door had slammed upon his visitor, and the face of the millionaire was blanched and old.

CHAPTER XXVI

Hember Street, Commercial Road, has long since been given over to the stranger within the gate. Great gaunt 'models', which are models in ugliness, models in cheerless drabness, but never models of what domestic comfort should be, raised their unshapely, lopsided heads to the grey skies, and between model and model are untidy doorways through which, all the time, pass in and out never-ending strings of ugly men and stodgy, vacant-faced children.

Here you may catch the sound of a dozen tongues; every language that is spoken from the Baltic to the Caspian, and from the Ural Mountains to the Finnish shore is repeated in the jibber-jabber of these uncleanly men and frowsy girl-women. The neighbourhood is for the most part populated by respectable and honest (if unsavoury) people, hard-working and industrious in a sense which the average working-class man of London would not understand, for it is an industry which rises at five and ends its work when smarting eyes and reeling brain make further effort impossible.

Yet there is a fair sprinkling of the Continental criminal classes to be found here, and Hermann Zeberlieff went armed to his interview. It was of his seeking. For some time past he had been under the impression that the house in Park Lane was being watched. He could not afford to bring Micheloff, that little pseudo-Frenchman with the blotchy face and the little eyes, to the notice of the watchers.

Without knocking Zeberlieff passed through an open door, along an uncarpeted hall, and mounted the stairs to the third floor of one of the houses.

He tapped on a door and a cheerful voice said: '*Entrez!*'

Micheloff, in his shirt sleeves, smoking a long, thin cigar, was neither heroic nor domestic. He was just commonplace.

'Come in!' he roared – his joviality was expressed in measure of sound. 'Come in, *mon vieux!*'

He dusted a rickety chair with great ostentation, but Hermann ignored the civility.

The room was large and simply furnished – a bed, a table, a couple of chairs, a couple of trunks well labelled, a picture of President Carnot and a little glass ikon over the mantelpiece seemed to make this place 'home' for Micheloff.

'Lock the door,' said Hermann. 'I have very important business, and I do not desire intrusion.'

Obediently the smaller man turned the key.

'My friend,' said Hermann, 'I have big work for you – the best work in the world so far as payment is concerned. There is a thousand pounds for you and another thousand for distribution amongst your friends – it is the last piece of work I shall ask you to do. If it succeeds I shall be beyond the necessity for your help; if I fail I shall be beyond its scope.'

'You shall succeed, my ancient,' said the short man, enthusiastically. 'I will work for you with greater fervour since now I know that you are one with me in spirit. Ah! pupil of Le Cinq!' he shook his finger in heavy jocularity. 'What shall we teach you that you cannot teach us?'

Hermann smiled. He was never indifferent to praise – even the praise of a confessed cut-throat. 'There must be no killing,' he said. 'I am through with that – even now the infernal police are continuing their inquiries into the death of the girl Gritter.'

'So much the better,' said the other heartily. 'I am a babe – these things distress me. I have a soft heart. I could weep.' There were tears in his eyes.

'Don't weep, you fool!'

Hermann hated weeping. It was another of his pet abominations. The sight of tears lashed him to frantic desperation.

Micheloff spread out his fat hands.

'Excellency!' he said with great impression, 'I do not weep.'

'Listen to me,' said Hermann, lowering his voice. 'Do you know King Kerry?'

The other nodded.

'You know his office?'

Micheloff shrugged his shoulders.

'Who does not know the office of the great King Kerry – the window, the mirrors, and the safe full of millions, *ma foi*?'

'You will find precious few millions there,' he said dryly. 'But you will find much that will be valuable to me.'

Micheloff looked dubious.

'It is a great undertaking,' he said – the conversation was in the staccato French of Marseilles – 'the guard – all the circumstances are against success. And the safe – it is combination – yes?'

Hermann nodded.

'Before it was combination,' said the other man regretfully, 'and there was a death regrettable.'

'I have reason to think that he changes the combination every week – it was probably changed yesterday. I will give you two. You may try –' A light came to his eyes. 'I wonder,' he said to himself, then slowly, 'try "Elsie".'

Micheloff nodded.

'That is but one,' he said.

'That is all I can give you now,' said Hermann, rising. 'If that fails you must use your blowpipe. I leave the details to you. Only this – I want a packet you will find marked "Private". Leave everything relating to the business, but bring all that is marked "Private".'

He left behind him two hundred pounds and Micheloff would have embraced him at the sight of the money, but the other pushed him back roughly.

'I do not like your Continental customs,' he said, and added, to appease the humiliated Russian, 'I have lost things like that.'

He went downstairs to the accompaniment of a roar of laughter. It was an excellent joke on Micheloff – he repeated it with discreet modification at his club that night.

The faithful man-servant, Martin, was waiting up when Hermann arrived home.

'Get me a strong cup of coffee, and go to bed,' he said.

He went up to his study and switched on the light and folded his coat over the back of a chair. It was one of his eccentricities that he valeted himself.

He drew a chair up to the desk and sat, his chin on his palm, looking vacantly before him until Martin came up with the coffee. 'Leave it and go to bed,' he said.

'What time in the morning, sir?' asked the man.

Hermann jerked his head impatiently. 'I will write the hour on the slate,' he said. He had a small porcelain slate affixed to his bedroom door to convey his belated instructions. He stirred his coffee mechanically, and drank it steaming hot. Then he addressed himself to the correspondence that awaited him. It was characteristic of him that, face to face with ruin as he was, he sent generous cheques to the appeals which came to him from hospitals and charitable institutions. The few letters he wrote in his big, sprawling handwriting were brief. Presently he had finished all that was necessary and he resumed his old attitude.

He remained thus till the church clock struck four, and then he passed into his bedroom, locking the door behind him.

CHAPTER XXVII

'Oh, Mr Kerry, You can make me merry; Buy me Trafalgar Square, I want to keep my chicken there! Oh, Mr Kerry, Just jot my wishes down; I can comb my moustache with the Marble Arch If you'll lend me London Town.'

It was gentle wit, but the great house roared with amusement at this latest addition to the gayest of the revues.

None laughed more heartily than Kerry in the shadow of the stage box. He was in the company of Elsie Marion, Vera Zeberlieff and Gordon Bray. Elsie Marion didn't know whether she approved, but the stately girl by her side laughed quietly.

'This is the last word in fame,' said Gordon Bray.

He sat at King Kerry's elbow, and was genuinely amused.

'How embarrassed the singer would be,' said Kerry with a little twinkle in his eye, 'if I stepped round to the stage door and offered him a conveyance of a slice of London.'

'When do you go away, sir?' It was Bray who asked the question. King Kerry turned his head and spoke over his shoulder.

'I want to get away at the end of the week,' he said. 'It is rather late for Marienbad, but I must be unfashionable. I am afraid I shall be away for a fortnight.'

'Afraid!' smiled Bray.

The millionaire nodded.

'Yes,' he said seriously, 'I do not really want to go away at all. The healthiest experience in life is to be interested in your work, and I have not yet grown stale.'

They saw the revue through to its pleasant end and adjourned for supper. Vera was a member of the Six Hundred Club, and to this exclusive establishment the party went. King Kerry seized the first opportunity to speak to Vera alone.

'I want to see you tomorrow,' he said. 'There is something very important I should like to discuss with you, something which I think you ought to know.'

His tone was so grave that the girl looked at him a little apprehensively. 'It is not Hermann again?' she asked.

He nodded. Something told her that he knew. 'It is to do with Hermann,' he said. 'I am afraid you have got just a little hurt coming – I would have spared you that, if I could.'

She shrugged her shoulders with a gesture of weariness.

'I can stand just one more,' she replied. 'I do not think you really know what life has been with Hermann.'

'I can guess,' he said grimly.

She recovered her spirits at supper, and made an excellent hostess, and Elsie, to whom this was a new and a beautiful world, had a most fascinating hour as the tango dancers glided and dipped between the gaily decorated tables.

The Six Hundred is the best of the night clubs. Duchesses order tables in advance and the most famous actresses of the world are members, and may be seen nightly in their precious toilettes seated about the little tables of the great dining-hall. Here was laughter and music and song, and the murmur and magic of life, the life of the leisured and the artistic – of the section of Bohemia which dresses for dinner.

Elsie watched the unaccustomed scenes, comforted by the light and the glitter. It was unlike anything she had ever seen before. No staring eyes surveyed them; the club was used to celebrities and even the whisper that the 'King of London' was in its midst aroused little more than passing interest.

Vera was sitting next to Kerry, and after the first course had been served she spoke to him under her breath.

'Hermann is here,' she said. 'He is sitting a little to your left and behind you.'

He nodded. 'I saw him come in,' he said. 'I do not anticipate any particular danger from him here.'

He looked at his watch.

'Oh, please do not think of going yet, Mr Kerry!' the girl begged.

'I am not going,' he said. 'But it is a practice of mine, as you know, to make a call at my office before I go home, and I was just wondering what was the hour.'

Hermann Zeberlieff had seen the action, and suddenly he rose, leaving the elegant Mr Hubbard, whose guest he was, without any apology and strolled across to the table.

A dead silence greeted him, but he was not in any way embarrassed. From where he stood, he could look down at King Kerry and his sister, and there was an ample display of good humour on his handsome face.

'Does anybody feel inclined,' he asked languidly, 'to do a little scientific hatchet-burying?'

He addressed the company at large. There was not one there against whom he had not offended. Elsie was ignorant perhaps of the part the man had played, but she looked up at him anxiously.

Gordon Bray, with the memory of drugged drink and an awakening in a certain wine cellar in Park Lane, went a dull red. King Kerry's face was expressionless, and it was only Vera who smiled gaily at the man who had neglected no effort to remove her from the world.

'Because,' Hermann went on, 'if at this particularly genial moment of life you feel inclined to accept me as your guest I am in a most humble frame of mind.'

It was a situation at once delicate and trying: Vera for the moment was deceived by his loneliness and looked a little pleadingly at King Kerry.

'Certainly,' he responded. 'Will you ask the waiter to put a chair for your brother?'

'What about your guest?' asked Vera.

Hermann shrugged his shoulders.

'He is waiting for somebody else,' he said, 'and he will be rather relieved than otherwise to get rid of me.'

It happened that he partly spoke the truth, because Hubbard was expecting Leete, who joined him a few minutes later. But since the two had foregathered to talk ways and means with the man who had so calmly deserted them, they found little consolation in one another's society.

Hermann was charming. Never before had King Kerry known him so gay, so cheerful, so full of sparkling wit, so ready with good-natured banter.

It was a new Hermann they saw – a suave, polished man of the world, versed in its niceties, its tone, and its standard of humour. He told stories that were new, had anecdotes that not one member of the party had heard before, which was strange: but never once did he address Kerry, though he blandly included Gordon Bray in his conversation whenever the opportunity offered.

That young man, resentful as he was, and with the memory of his unpleasant experience behind him, found himself engaged in an animated conversation with this man who had treated him so badly.

The coffee stage had long since come and gone. King Kerry fidgeted uneasily, he did not like late hours, and he still had a little work to do at the office. Late nights disorganized the following day, for he laid down an irreducible minimum of seven hours for sleep.

Still Hermann rattled on, and they were forced against their will to listen and be amused.

Martin Hubbard had long since gone with Leete, and Hermann had met their scowls with his most pleasant smile. They were out of the scheme for the moment.

The tables began to thin a little; the more sedate members had gathered up their belongings and departed in a cloud of chatter and laughter.

Vera's table was one of the last four occupied in the room.

'I really think we must go now,' said Kerry. 'It is nearly three o'clock.'

They rose, Hermann with an apology.

'I'm afraid I have kept you,' he said.

Kerry returned a conventional and polite reply.

It was whilst Vera was settling the bill that young Lord Fallingham, whom King Kerry knew slightly, came in with a most hilarious party.

He was settling upon a table when he caught sight of the millionaire and came over.

'How do you do, Mr King Kerry?' he said cordially. 'I congratulate you on the fruition of your scheme, and I only regret that the successful conclusion of your business has removed so picturesque a spectacle from London.'

'Meaning me?' asked King Kerry good humouredly.

'Meaning your Jewel House,' said the young man.

King Kerry shook his head.

'It will be a long time before the Jewel House departs,' he said. 'The one concrete evidence of the Trust's existence will remain for many years.'

The young man looked down at him a little bewildered.

'But you are moving from Glasshouse Street,' he persisted. 'I went round there to find you tonight; I have just come from there.'

'You have just come from there?' repeated Kerry in astonishment.

'Yes. I have a man here,' he jerked his head towards his table, 'who is home from India, and I took him round to see the wonderful sights, and, alas! there were no longer wonderful sights to be seen.'

'Exactly what do you mean?' King Kerry's voice was sharp and commanding. 'I have not moved from Glasshouse Street.'

'I do not quite understand you,' said Fallingham slowly. 'The place is in darkness, and you have two huge bills pasted up on the window outside saying that your office is removed to 106, Piccadilly Circus.'

For a moment Elsie's startled eyes met the millionaire's, then he turned quickly to the smiling Hermann.

'I see,' he said, without raising his voice.

'Exactly, Mr King Kerry, what do you see?' drawled the other.

'I understand your intrusion into this party,' said King Kerry, 'and your entertaining conversation is explained.'

With an excuse he left them and hurried downstairs.

He hailed the first taxi-cab he could see and drove to his office. The shop front was in darkness; he peered through, but could not see the safe. Once the lights were out, as they had not been since the opening of the Jewel House, the safe would be in the shadow.

He unlocked the outer door and entered, pressing over the switch on the left of the door. But no light resulted. He went out again into the street and called the nearest policeman.

'This place has been burgled,' he said.

'Burgled, sir! Why I thought you had moved your furniture tonight.'

'Who put those bills up?'

King Kerry pointed to the large printed notice on the window.

'I don't know,' said the man. 'When I came on duty the shop was in darkness and these bills were posted. Naturally, when I saw there was no light I acted according to the instructions the police had received from you, and went across, but seeing the bills I thought it was all right.'

He whistled two of his mates, and the four men entered the building, the policemen flashing their lamps before them. In the commissionaire's box they found the unfortunate guard whose duty it was to protect the treasures of the safe. He was unconscious. He had been clubbed into insensibility, gagged and bound. The arrival of the relief only came just in time to save his life.

The commissionaire was nowhere to be seen. They found him afterwards in the smaller office, treated in very much the same way as his assistant. The only account he could give was that suddenly, while he was sitting in his box, something had been squirted in his face, something that had taken away his breath.

'I think it was ammonia,' he said, and that, before he could struggle or cry, he was knocked down, and awoke to find himself strung and gagged in the little office.

An examination of the place showed that all the electric light cables were cut. Possibly the burglary had been committed at the very moment when the police were changing over.

There was no necessity to unlock the steel door leading from the inner office to the safe room, the lock had been burnt out and the safe was open wide, and was apparently uninjured.

King Kerry uttered a smothered exclamation.

'Lend me your lamp,' he said, and rapidly examined the contents of the safe. None of the documents affecting the Trust had been disturbed, or if they had been moved they had been put back as they had been found. One bundle of envelopes, the most important to him, had gone.

'You had better report this,' he said, after a long silence. 'I will get somebody in to repair the damage to the electric cable.'

He sat in the inner office with no more light than a candle afforded, and there Elsie found him. Alarmed by the look on the millionaire's face, she had followed. 'Is anything gone?' she asked.

'A bundle of mine,' he said quietly; 'but, fortunately, nothing belonging to the business has been touched.'

'Are you sure your bundle has gone?' she asked.

It was a true woman's question, the inevitable expression of distrust in man's power of search. He smiled slightly. 'You had better look for yourself,' he said. 'There is a lamp over there.'

She went into the office; the safe was still open and she was carefully examining the contents before she remembered that she did not know what she was seeking.

She went back to Kerry. 'It is a bunch of long envelopes,' he said, 'inscribed "Relating to the affairs of King Kerry – Private".'

She nodded and went back. She turned over every envelope in the safe without making any discovery. Then she flashed her lamp over the floor. Here she found something: One long, thin envelope, carefully sealed, had fallen, and lay on its edge against the side of the safe, kept in its upright position possibly by the edge of the carpet.

She picked it up and, turning the lantern light upon it, read –

'Marriage Certificate of King Kerry and Henrietta Zeberlieff.'

The girl stared at the envelope.

Zeberlieff! Hermann's sister!

CHAPTER XXVIII

'*Voilà*!' said Micheloff.

He stood in an attitude of complete satisfaction, his arms akimbo, and the bundle of envelopes, tightly bound with string, which lay upon the desk testified mutely to the skill of the man.

There were two red patches on Hermann's cheeks and his eyes blazed with triumph. 'At last! You are a wonderful man,' he said ironically.

Micheloff shrugged his shoulders.

'It was nothing,' he said. 'The genius of the idea; the fore-thought was all yours, oh, *mon générale*! Who but you would have thought of the bills to paste upon the windows? That was a master stroke; the rest was easy.'

'You had to cut out the lock, I suppose?' asked Hermann as he untied the strings which bound the letters.

Micheloff shook his great head. 'It was simple. Here again your perception!' He extended his arms admiringly.

'My perception!' said the other roughly. 'Did you open the safe with the name I gave?' The man bowed his head. 'With "Elsie"?' Again Micheloff nodded.

The brows of Hermann Zeberlieff were knitted, his under-jaw stuck out pugnaciously, and he was not beautiful to look upon at the moment.

'Elsie,' he repeated, 'damn him! I'll make him sorry for that.'

He cut the cord impatiently and sorted over the envelopes.

'You have missed one,' he said.

'Impossible,' replied the calm Micheloff. 'I examined with great care, and my knowledge of English is almost perfect. Every one is here.'

'There was one which contained a marriage certificate,' said Hermann.

'That is there also,' said the other. 'I particularly remember placing it there.'

'It is not here now.' He made another search. 'You fool, you have left behind the most valuable letter of all.'

'It is a thousand pities,' said Micheloff a little impatiently. He was tired of criticism, tired of being bullied. He wanted a little praise for the risk he had taken and the work he had done.

'Nevertheless,' he said, 'I think that you have sufficient for your money.'

Hermann thought a moment, and went to a little safe in the wall, opened it, and took out a bundle of notes. He carefully counted ten and handed them to his tool, who counted them again no less carefully. 'This is exactly half what you promised,' he said.

'There is exactly all there that you will get,' said Hermann. 'You have failed to secure what I asked for, what I particularly desired you to bring to me.'

'I require another thousand pounds,' said Micheloff; his little eyes twinkled coldly. 'I desire another thousand pounds, *monsieur*, and I do not leave here until I get it.'

'You will go!' Hermann took a step towards him and stopped.

Micheloff was taking no chances that night. He had felt the strangling white hands of the other about his throat, and it was an experience which he did not intend should be repeated. Hermann stopped before the black barrel of a Browning pistol.

'No, no, my ancient!' said Micheloff. 'We will have no further exhibition from the pupil of Le Cinq!'

'Put that revolver down!' cried Hermann. 'You fool, put it down!'

He was terribly agitated: in a state of panic almost. He feared firearms to an extraordinary extent, and even Micheloff was astounded at the pallor and the shakiness of the man. Something that was human in the little Russian made him drop his hand.

Hermann wiped his brow and licked his dry lips. 'Do not ever lift a pistol to me again,' he said hoarsely. 'I cannot stand it. It is one of the things I hate worse than anything else in the world.'

He went to the safe again and counted ten more notes with trembling fingers and threw them down on the table.

'Take them!' he said.

Micheloff took them, and without stopping to count them made his way to the door.

'My friend,' he said elaborately, 'I salute – and retire!'

And now Hermann Zeberlieff was alone.

Very carefully he examined the contents of the envelopes. One of them containing a bundle of correspondence afforded him some quiet amusement – the letters were in his own writing.

He read them through again and again and carefully burnt them. He had lit a fire in his study with this object. There was one envelope which he did not touch, inscribed with the name of a girl who had loved him and who had learnt his secret with horror, and in all the frenzy of her despair had taken her own life.

He turned the envelope over and over – something prevented him from examining its contents.

His chin upon his palm, he sat thinking, and then the recollection of Micheloff's words came to him, and he sat bolt upright in his chair.

'Elsie,' he repeated, and his lips curled in a sneer. So that was it – this man had fallen in love with a gutter-child he had found in London. She was enough in his thoughts, sufficient in his life to be entrusted with his secrets. This girl had all that Hermann Zeberlieff desired – once he had had the opportunity of standing next to King Kerry, first in place amongst his friends, trusted, and growing to fortune as the millionaire had grown. He had thrown it away, and this girl had taken all that he had scorned.

A petty thought, perhaps; but a natural thought.

Only one envelope remained to be examined. Upon his judgement as to whether its contents should prove as he had anticipated depended his future.

He had given a brief glance at the inscription on the envelope. So far he was satisfied that he had not been at fault – the envelope bore the words, 'Relating to my marriage'.

He cleared all the other papers away and locked them in a drawer of his desk and opened the one remaining.

It contained twenty sheets of foolscap, closely written. He read steadily, turning the sheets as he came to them, till he reached the passage he sought. He had expected to find it in another form, and was momentarily dismayed to find that the envelope contained no more than this one statement that he was now reading.

But the paragraph cleared up all doubt in his mind – he read it again and again, slowly absorbing its sense until he could have repeated it by heart.

It ran –

'My marriage was a disaster. It will be understood why from the foregoing. Henrietta's mother had died in a lunatic asylum. I did not know this before the marriage. The mother had imparted something of her strong will and her strong character, with an utter irresponsibility peculiar to her wild nature, to her daughter...

'She was extraordinarily ignorant as to the law of the United States, and this had probably led her to commit the crime which she had committed – for her daughter's sake. When I discovered Henrietta's duplicity, when I awoke to a full realization of her terrible and absorbing passion, when I realized how absolutely impossible such a marriage was, I saw in what a terrible position I had placed myself. I did not love Henrietta; I do not think that in any time of my life she had aroused the confidence and the trust which is the basis of love. I had been fascinated by the glamour of a beautiful woman, had been swept off my feet by her exotic beauty – she was little more than a child in those days.

'I consulted my lawyer. I had made my ante-nuptial arrangements, and had settled upon her, in the terms of my will, ten million dollars upon my death. I now desired earnestly to see how far I was bound by that contract.

'I had no wish to rob her other inheritance, though a large portion of her mother's estate would come to her, and she would not have felt the loss had I been able to cancel my marriage contract, but the lawyers informed me that it would be impossible, without a great deal of publicity, which I did not desire, and even then there was some doubt as to whether I should succeed.

'It is a terrible thought that this woman will so benefit by my death – terrible, because I am confident that Hermann Zeberlieff would not hesitate to destroy me if he knew that Henrietta would benefit.'

Hermann read the sheet through and folded it with a little smile. 'You are perfectly right, my friend. Henrietta has a very loyal brother.'

He locked up the document in the safe and stood cogitating by the fireplace.

'I wonder why I hate firearms,' he said, half to himself, 'because it seems to me that is the only method which is now available.

'Out you go!' he waved his hand to the ceiling. 'Out you go, my King Kerry, deserter of wives, and maker of wills! I have learnt from your own lips the necessity for your destruction – poor Henrietta.' He smiled again.

Where was this wife of Kerry's?

Hermann knew – very well he knew.

But Elsie, who tossed restlessly, sleeplessly, from side to side in her tumbled bed in Chelsea, thought and thought and thought again without coming any nearer to a solution of the business.

The morning sun streamed into her room to find her awake and still thinking.

CHAPTER XXIX

'You wanted to see me, Mr Kerry?'

Vera was looking beautiful that morning, Kerry thought. She reminded him somewhat of her sister – her sister as she had been at her best.

Yet there was a quality in her face that Henrietta had never had – a softness, a humanity, a kindness, which was foreign to the older woman's nature.

'Yes, I want to speak to you,' he said. 'I am going into some of your family history, if you don't mind.'

'That's rather alarming,' she smiled. 'Which side of my family, in particular?'

He hesitated.

'To be exact, the only branch it touches is your father, and even he is only a passive agent.'

'You are speaking of Hermann's mother?' she said quickly.

He nodded.

'Did you ever hear of her?'

The girl shook her head.

'I have heard rather terrible stories about her,' she said slowly. 'She was in a lunatic asylum for a number of years. Poor papa! – it must have been terrible for him.'

'It was,' said King Kerry. 'Even I am not old enough to remember all that happened. She was a remarkable woman,' he went on, plunging into the business of his visit. 'She was a Pole, a very beautiful girl. Her father and a large family emigrated from Poland to America in the sixties, and she met him when she was little more than a child. I have reason to believe that the family had come from noble stock, but, if you do not mind my speaking very plainly –'

'I would prefer it,' said Vera.

'They were a pretty decadent lot.'

She nodded her head.

'I know that,' she said with a half-smile.

'Hermann's mother had many remarkable ideas, even as a child, and perhaps the most remarkable of all was one which led to a great deal of unhappiness.'

He hesitated.

'Do you know that you have a half-sister?'

The girl's eyebrows rose.

'A half-sister?' she said incredulously. 'No, I did not – it is news to me.'

'I married her,' he said simply.

She looked at him with wondering eyes. For a moment neither of them spoke.

'I married her,' he went on. 'I met her in Denver City. She had gone West on a trip to her relatives and I was pretty young and headstrong in those days. I met her at a ball, and became engaged to her the same night, and was married to her within a week.'

He paced up and down the room with his hands behind him.

'It is only right to say,' he said slowly, 'that that marriage, from the very moment when we left the justice's parlour where we had been formally united, was a hideous mistake – a mistake which might very well have embittered the whole of my life. The shadow of Henrietta Zeberlieff has hung over me for fifteen years, and there have been times when life had been unendurable.'

She was silent.

It was so startling, so extraordinary, that even now she could not grasp it. This marriage offered an explanation for much. She looked at her brother-in-law enviously. How strange the relationship seemed! She felt a sudden glow of loving kindness toward one who had suffered at the hands of her own flesh and blood.

'Is she still alive?' she asked.

Kerry nodded.

'She is still alive,' he said.

'Hermann knows?' the girl said quickly.

He nodded his head.

'And he is concealing her, keeping her in the background. Is she mad, too?'

King Kerry considered a moment. 'I think she is,' he said.

'How terrible.'

The pain on the girl's face was pitiable to the man. 'Can't I go to her? Can't I see her?'

He shook his head. 'You could do no good,' he said. 'You must wait developments. I meant to have told you more, but somehow – it has stuck in my throat. Last night, as you know, a burglary was committed at my office and the documents relating to my wife were stolen. I have my own idea as to why they were stolen, but I thought it possible that within the next few days you would come to learn what I have told you and perhaps more. It is fairer to you that I should prepare you for the shock.'

He picked up his hat. The girl came towards him, her eyes filled with tears and laid her two hands on his.

'I thought –' She looked at him steadily.

'What do you think, Miss Zeberlieff?'

'I thought,' she said, with a little catch in her voice, 'that Elsie –'

He nodded.

'I wish to God it were so,' he said, in a low tone. 'Money isn't everything, is it?' He made a pathetic attempt to smile.

'It isn't everything,' she said, in a low voice. 'I think the only thing worth while in life is love.'

He nodded. 'Thank God, you have found it,' he said; and, raising her face to his, he kissed her on the cheek. 'After all,' he smiled, 'you are my sister-in-law. That is a liberty which my remote relationship completely exonerates.'

He went back to his club to lunch, for he was in no mood to meet Elsie. The very sight of her brought a little twinge of pain to his heart. He loved this girl very dearly. She had grown to him as a delicate flower might grow in the shade of a plant of sturdier growth for protection and comfort.

His mind dwelt upon her as he sat at his lunch, and her beautiful eyes, the perfect oval of her face, the little pout of red lips.

He shook his head – there was no way out that he could see.

He finished lunch, and stood for a moment on the steps of the club, then hailed a taxi. Just as he was stepping into the cab a District messenger-boy had entered the club and the chauffeur was driving off when a club servant came flying down the steps with a letter.

'This has just arrived, sir,' he said.

King Kerry opened it and read – 'For the last time, I want you to see me. I am sailing for South America tomorrow to retrieve my fortunes. Come to Park Lane. There is nothing to fear.'

'"For the last time,"' repeated King Kerry. He crushed the letter and put it in his pocket, and turning to the club waiter – 'There is no answer,' he said. 'Tell the driver to go to 410, Park Lane.'

CHAPTER XXX

'So you've come?' said Hermann.

'For the last time,' said the other.

'Assuredly' – then – 'What is that?' Hermann asked quickly.

King Kerry had laid down upon the table a newspaper he had purchased on his way. He had been suspicious of Hermann's intentions, and had bought the journal to learn the sailing dates and to discover whether the South American mail sailed the following day.

It happened that, as far as he could gather from a perusal of the shipping-list, Zeberlieff had spoken the truth.

Hermann snatched up the paper, his face was drawn and haggard of a sudden. Over his shoulder the millionaire read in the largest headlines –

SHOOTING AFFRAY IN WHITECHAPEL
WELL-KNOWN ANARCHIST ARRESTED
ASSAILANT MAKES FULL CONFESSION

Hermann read the lines rapidly. The arrested man was Micheloff – and he would tell – everything. Everything would come out now, the little Russian would not hesitate to implicate anybody and everybody to save his own skin or to bring about a mitigation of his sentence.

So he made a full confession! Of what! The paper only had the brief and most guarded account: 'The prisoner made a long statement, which was being investigated,' said the journal, and went on to explain that the police sought the owner of a large sum of money which was found upon the prisoner.

So it was all out. He threw down the paper on the table. The game was up. He was at his last desperate throw, and then 'Farewell, Hermann Zeberlieff!'

'That has upset you rather?' said King Kerry. He had skimmed the account on his way to the house.

'It doesn't upset me so very much,' said the other. 'It alters my plans a little – it may very easily alter yours. I have very little time.' He looked at his watch. Kerry saw a packed bag and an overcoat on a chair, and guessed that Zeberlieff was making immediate preparations for departure.

'But that little time,' Hermann went on, 'must be profitably spent. For the last time, King Kerry, will you help me?'

'With money? No! How often have I helped you, and invariably you have employed the assistance I have given you to combat me?'

'I want exactly a million,' said the other. 'I am going away to South America, where there is ample scope for a gentleman of enterprise.'

'You will get nothing from me.'

'Reconsider your decision – now!'

Kerry turned. A revolver covered him.

'Reconsider it, or you're a dead man!' said Zeberlieff, calmly. 'I tell you I am in desperate straits. I must get out of this country today – unless you stand by me – not only with money, but in every other way –'

There was a loud knock at the door below. Zeberlieff's haggard face went white, yet he edged to the window and looked out. Three men, unmistakable policemen in plain clothes, were standing about the door.

'This is the end,' said Zeberlieff, and fired.

As he did so, King Kerry sprang forward and knocked up his arm. The two closed, the white hands sought for his throat, but Kerry knew the other's strength – and weakness.

There was a sharp scuffle, but Zeberlieff was powerless in his arms. He swung him round as the door burst open and two men dashed in.

Before they could grasp their prisoner he had stooped to the floor and picked up the revolver that had fallen in the struggle. There was a quick report, and, with that little smile which was particularly Hermann Zeberlieff's, he collapsed sideways on to the floor.

Kerry went down on his knees by his side and lifted the fallen head.

'Hullo, Kingy!' coughed the dying Hermann. 'This is pretty lucky for you – you and your Elsie!'

A frown gathered over the fast-glazing eyes, and it was with that frown on that handsome face that Hermann Zeberlieff went to the Judge Who knows all things.

One of the policemen leant over him.

'He's dead!' he said as he loosened the shirt about the neck of the silent figure.

He stood up sharply.

'My God!' he gasped. 'It's a woman!'

King Kerry nodded.

'My wife,' he said, and looked down at the dead woman at his feet.

* * * * *

'I had never suspected it – never.' Vera's eyes showed signs of tears. 'And yet, now I come to think of it, she never allowed me in her room, never allowed a servant to valet her, and there are lots of little things I can remember which might have aroused my suspicion.'

'It was her mother's fault,' said King Kerry. 'Her mother was ignorant of the laws of the United States, and was under the impression that your father's estate would go automatically to a son, and that a daughter had no powers of inheritance. She craved for that son, and when Henrietta arrived, the poor soul was distracted. The doctor was bribed to certify the child as a boy, and her aunt and her mother brought her up as a boy. She was assisted in this deception by Henrietta's character – for Henrietta had a man's way and a man's reason. She was a man in this, that she had neither pity nor remorse. She allowed a beautiful girl to fall in love with her without letting her know her secret. When it was discovered the girl committed suicide – you probably know the circumstances.'

'I know,' said the faltering Vera. 'But I thought –'

'Everybody thought that,' said Kerry. 'One other aunt was frightened and had the girl sent to her at Denver – she had a farm there. She allowed her hair to grow and dressed her as a girl – it was there that I met her and married her.

'But the fascination of the old life – she had got into a speculating set on Wall Street – was too much for her.

'She wanted to be thought a man, to hear her business abilities and her genius praised – as a man. She made one or two very wise speculations which were her undoing. She left me and went back to Wall Street. I pleaded with her, but there was nothing to be gained by appealing to Henrietta's better instincts. She laughed. The next day she turned a "corner" against me – she smashed my market – with my money,' he added grimly. 'I did not mind that, one can always get money, but she pursued it. I was a "bear" in corn, pulling the prices down; she and her friends "cornered" the world's supply, so she thought. I smashed her and gave her a million to start afresh, but she hated me from that moment and pursued me with malignant –' He stopped. 'God help her!' he said sadly. 'God help all women – good or bad!'

'Amen,' said Vera Zeberlieff.

* * * * *

King Kerry came to see Elsie two months later. He arrived unexpectedly at Geneva, where she was holiday-making, and she met him upon Quai des Alpes, and was staggered at the sight of him.

He was young again – the lines were gone from his face – the lines of care and memory – and his eyes were bright with health.

'I have just come along from Chamonix,' he said. 'I have been fixing up a villa.'

'Are you going to live there?' she asked in consternation.

He shook his head smilingly.

A carriage drove past, and she had some work to restrain a smile.

'Who is that?' he asked.

'Do you remember Mr Hubbard?'

He nodded. He remembered the 'Beauty' very well.

'He has married the most dreadful woman. And they have come here on their honeymoon,' she said.

He nodded again.

'His landlady,' he said grimly. 'That's poetic justice.'

'But the most poetical of all the pieces of justice,' she laughed, 'is that Vera and Mr Bray are staying at the same hotel on their honeymoon.'

'That is rough luck,' admitted King Kerry with a smile, 'and as you say, horribly just.'

'It is rather terrible, though,' she said, 'the number of honeymoon folks who are in Geneva.'

He took her by the arm and walked her along the quay.

'We shall not add to the number,' he said. 'We will go to Chamonix.'

'When?' asked the girl faintly.

'Next week,' said King Kerry.

'I love Chamonix,' she said after a while. 'It is so splendid – Mont Blanc with his white smooth head always above you. I wish we could take Mont Blanc to England with us,' she added whimsically.

'I'll ask the price of it,' said the Man who Bought London.

BIOGRAPHICAL NOTE

Richard Horatio Edgar Wallace was born in London on 1 April 1875, the son of a widowed actress. He was fostered by a fish porter at Billingsgate market and his wife, and later adopted by them.

Having left school at the age of twelve, he began his working life by selling newspapers at Ludgate Circus near Fleet Street. At the age of twenty-one, Wallace joined the army but transferred as swiftly as possible to the Royal Army Medical Corps. It was not until he finally transferred again to the Press Corps and he began writing, that he at last found his calling.

During the Boer War, he worked as a war correspondent for the *Daily Mail*, as well as publishing poems and columns in various newspapers. He would go on to write over 170 novels, 18 stage plays and 957 short stories. Famously prolific, it has been estimated that one in four books read in the UK in 1928 was written by Wallace. He remains known today for his thrilling tales and for writing the early screenplay to the enduring classic film, *King Kong*.

Wallace died in Los Angeles in 1932, survived by his second wife and four children.

HESPERUS PRESS

Under our three imprints, Hesperus Press publishes over 300 books by many of the greatest figures in worldwide literary history, as well as contemporary and debut authors well worth discovering.

Hesperus Classics handpicks the best of worldwide and translated literature, introducing forgotten and neglected books to new generations.

Hesperus Nova showcases quality contemporary fiction and non-fiction designed to entertain and inspire.

Hesperus Minor rediscovers well-loved children's books from the past – these are books which will bring back fond memories for adults, which they will want to share with their children and loved ones.

To find out more visit **www.hesperuspress.com**

@HesperusPress

SELECTED TITLES FROM HESPERUS PRESS

Author	Title	Foreword writer
Adler-Olsen, Jussi	*Alphabet House*	
Alcott, Louisa May	*Good Wives*	
Alcott, Louisa May	*Jo's Boys*	
Alcott, Louisa May	*Little Men*	
Alcott, Louisa May	*Little Women*	
Arlt, Roberto	*Mad Toy, The*	Colm Tóibín
Austen, Jane	*Lady Susan*	
Austen, Jane	*Love and Friendship*	Fay Weldon
Austen, Jane	*Sanditon*	A.C. Grayling
Bannalec, Jean-Luc	*Death in Pont-Aven*	
Baum, Frank L.	*Emerald City of Oz, The*	
Baum, Frank L.	*Glinda of Oz*	
Baum, Frank L.	*Marvellous Land of Oz, The*	
Baum, Frank L.	*Wonderful Wizard of Oz, The*	
Benson, E.F.	*Mapp & Lucia*	
Biggers, Earl Derr	*Love Insurance*	
Börjlind, Cilla and Rolf	*Spring Tide*	
Brinton, Sybil	*Old Friends and New Fancies*	
Bronte, Charlotte	*Professor, The*	
Cather, Willa	*O Pioneers*	
Collins, Wilkie	*Frozen Deep, The*	
Conan Doyle, Arthur	*Poison Belt, The*	Matthew Sweet
Conan Doyle, Arthur	*Tragedy of the Korosko, The*	Tony Robinson
Conrad, Joseph	*Heart of Darkness*	A.N. Wilson
Dickens, Charles	*Chimes, The*	

Author	Title	Foreword writer
Dickens, Charles	*Haunted House, The*	Peter Ackroyd
Dickens, Charles	*Holly-Tree Inn, The*	
Dickens, Charles	*House to Let, A*	
Dickens, Charles	*Mrs Lirriper*	Philip Hensher
Dickens, Charles	*Mugby Junction*	Robert Macfarlane
Dickens, Charles	*Round of Stories by the Christmas Fire, A*	D.J. Taylor
Dickens, Charles	*Seven Poor Travellers, The*	
Dickens, Charles & Collins, Wilkie	*Perils of Certain English Prisoners, The*	
Dostoevsky, Fyodor	*Notes from the Underground*	Will Self
Eliot, George	*Janet's Repentance*	Kathryn Hughes
Eliot, George	*Mr Gilfil's Love Story*	Kirsty Gunn
Fitzgerald, F. Scott	*Popular Girl, The*	Helen Dunmore
Fitzgerald, F. Scott	*Rich Boy, The*	John Updike
Flaubert, Gustave	*Three Tales*	Margaret Drabble
Forster, E.M.	*Arctic Summer*	Anita Desai
Forster, E.M.	*Obelisk, The*	Amit Chaudhuri
Gara, Nathalie and Ladislas	*Welcome to the Free Zone*	Norman Lebrecht
Garnett, David	*Lady Into Fox*	John Burnside
Gaskell, Elizabeth	*Mr Harrison's Confession*	
Gaskell, Elizabeth	*Moorland Cottage, The*	
Gibbon, Lewis Grassic	*Spartacus*	
Goethe, Johann Wolfgang von	*Madwoman on a Pilgrimage, The*	Lewis Crofts
Goethe, Johann Wolfgang von	*Man of Fifty, The*	A.S. Byatt
Greene, Graham	*No Man's Land*	David Lodge

Author	Title	Foreword writer
Hastings, Milo M.	*City of Endless Night*	
Hawthorne, Nathaniel	*Rappaccini's Daughter*	Simon Schama
Hiltunen, Pekka	*Cold Courage*	
Hiltunen, Pekka	*Black Noise*	
James, Henry	*Diary of a Man of Fifty, The*	David Lodge
James, Henry	*In the Cage*	Libby Purves
James, Henry	*Lesson of the Master, The*	Colm Tóibín
Jonasson, Jonas	*Hundred-Year-Old Man Who Climbed Out of the Window and Disappeared, The*	
Kafka, Franz	*Metamorphosis*	Martin Jarvis
Kafka, Franz	*Trial, The*	Zadie Smith
Keilson, Hans	*Comedy in a Minor Key*	
London, Jack	*Before Adam*	
London, Jack	*People of the Abyss, The*	Alexander Masters
London, Jack	*Scarlet Plague, The*	Tony Robinson
London, Jack	*Sea-wolf, The*	
Montgomery, L. M.	*Tangled Web, A*	
Montgomery, L.M.	*Blue Castle, The*	
Nokes, David	*Nightingale Papers, The*	
Parks, Tim	*Talking About It*	
Puenzo, Lucía	*Wakolda*	
Roberts, Elizabeth Madox	*Time of Man, The*	
Roth, Joseph	*Hotel Savoy*	
Sackville-West, Vita	*Heir, The*	
Sade, Marquis de	*Betrayal*	John Burnside
Sade, Marquis de	*Virtue*	
Safier, David	*Apocalypse Next Tuesday*	

Author	Title	Foreword writer
Shaw, Bernard	*Adventures of the Black Girl in her Search for God, The*	Colm Tóibín
Starobinets, Anna	*Living, The*	
Stevenson, Robert Louis	*Dr Jekyll and Mr Hyde*	Helen Dunmore
Stjernström, Peter	*Best Book in the World, The*	
Thériault, Denis	*Peculiar Life of a Lonely Postman, The*	
Tolstoy, Leo	*Confession, A*	Helen Dunmore
Twain, Mark	*Diary of Adam and Eve, The*	John Updike
Vallgren, Carl-Johan	*Merman, The*	
Von Kleist, Heinrich	*Marquise of O–, The*	Andrew Miller
Walpole, Horace	*Castle of Otranto, The*	
Wilde, Oscar	*Canterville Ghost, The*	
Wilkie Collins	*Frozen Deep, The*	Andrew Smith
Woolf, Virginia	*Memoirs of a Novelist*	
Zola, Emile	*For a Night of Love*	A.N. Wilson